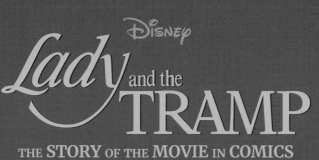

Disney

Lady and the TRAMP

THE STORY OF THE MOVIE IN COMICS

DARK HORSE BOOKS

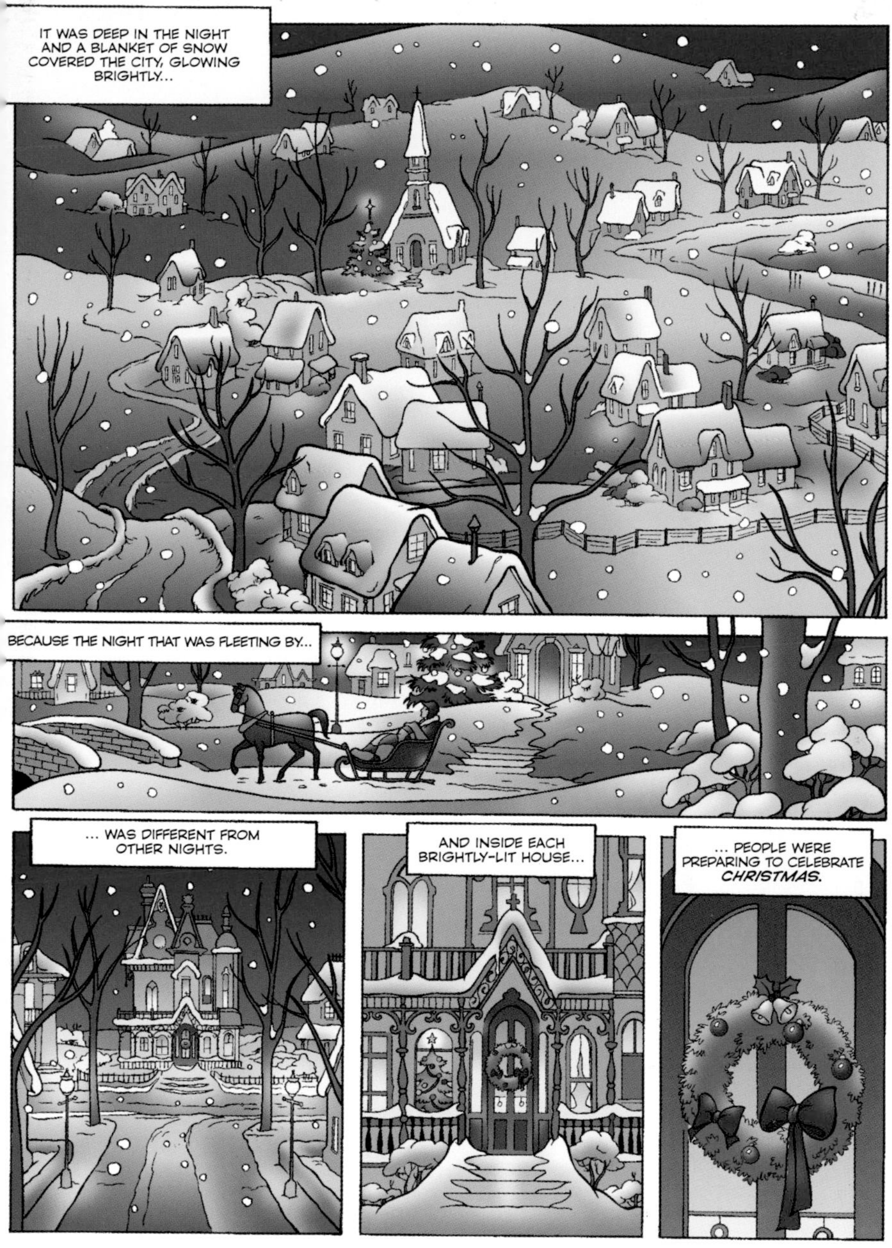
IT WAS DEEP IN THE NIGHT AND A BLANKET OF SNOW COVERED THE CITY, GLOWING BRIGHTLY...
BECAUSE THE NIGHT THAT WAS FLEETING BY...
... WAS DIFFERENT FROM OTHER NIGHTS.
AND INSIDE EACH BRIGHTLY-LIT HOUSE...
... PEOPLE WERE PREPARING TO CELEBRATE *CHRISTMAS.*

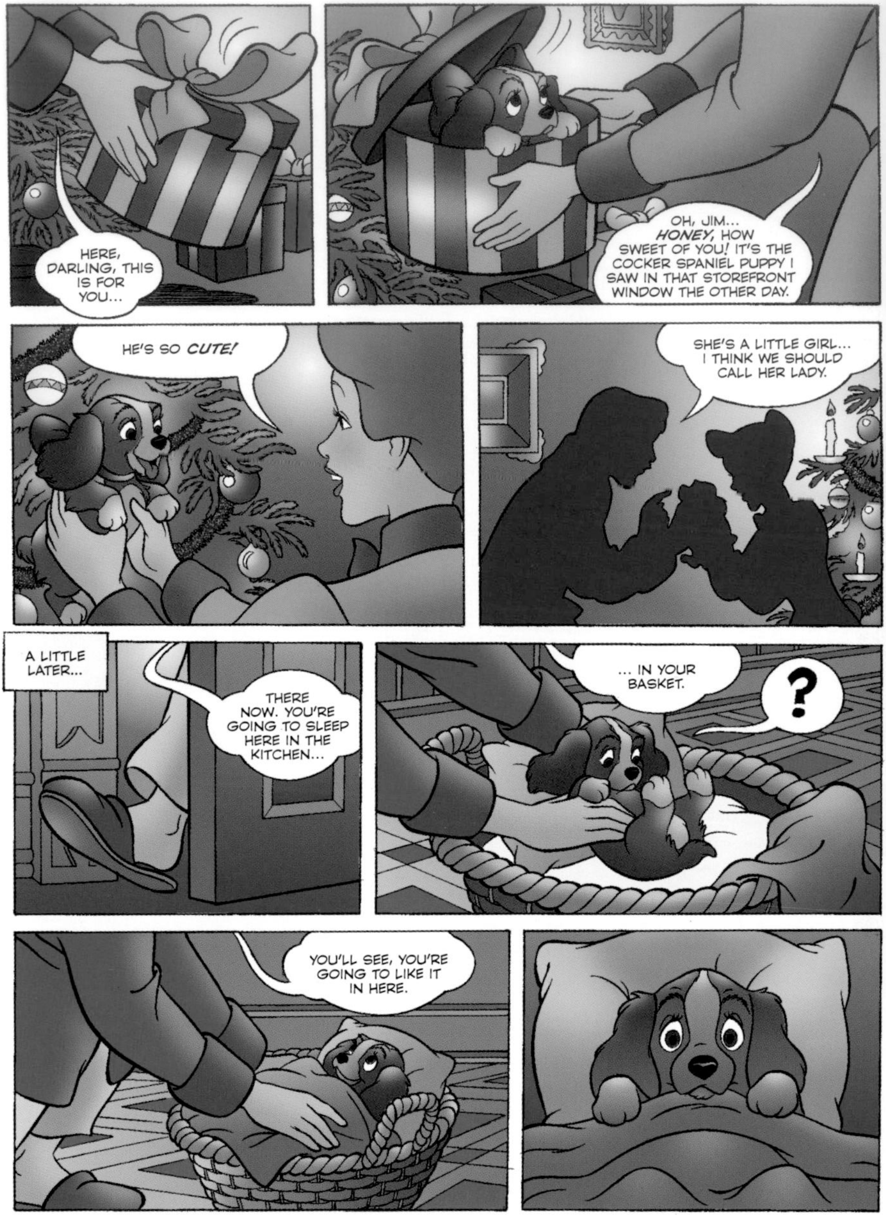

HERE, DARLING, THIS IS FOR YOU...
OH, JIM... HONEY, HOW SWEET OF YOU! IT'S THE COCKER SPANIEL PUPPY I SAW IN THAT STOREFRONT WINDOW THE OTHER DAY.
HE'S SO CUTE!
SHE'S A LITTLE GIRL... I THINK WE SHOULD CALL HER LADY.
A LITTLE LATER...
THERE NOW. YOU'RE GOING TO SLEEP HERE IN THE KITCHEN...
... IN YOUR BASKET.
?
YOU'LL SEE, YOU'RE GOING TO LIKE IT IN HERE.

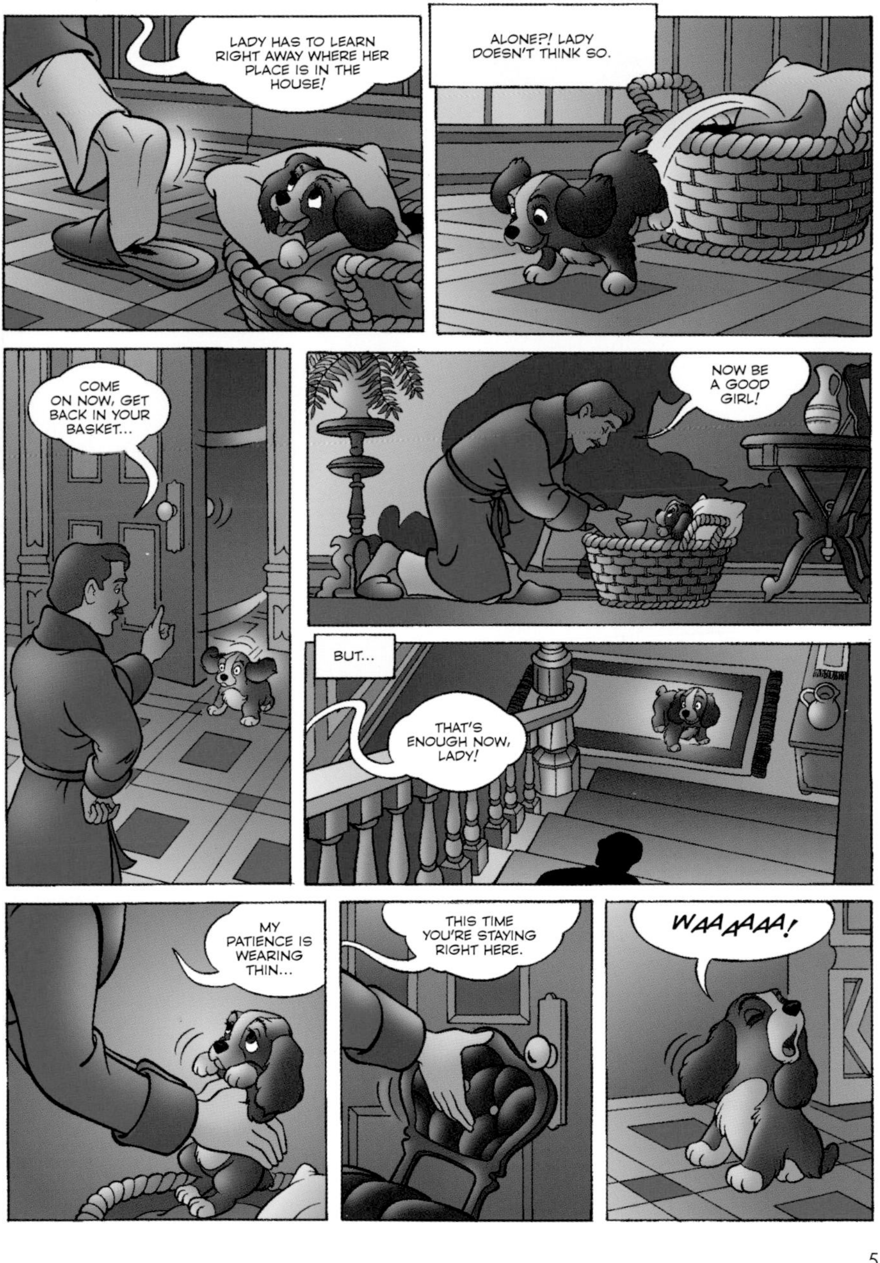
LADY HAS TO LEARN RIGHT AWAY WHERE HER PLACE IS IN THE HOUSE!
ALONE?! LADY DOESN'T THINK SO.
COME ON NOW, GET BACK IN YOUR BASKET...
NOW BE A GOOD GIRL!
BUT...
THAT'S ENOUGH NOW, LADY!
MY PATIENCE IS WEARING THIN...
THIS TIME YOU'RE STAYING RIGHT HERE.
WAAAAAA!

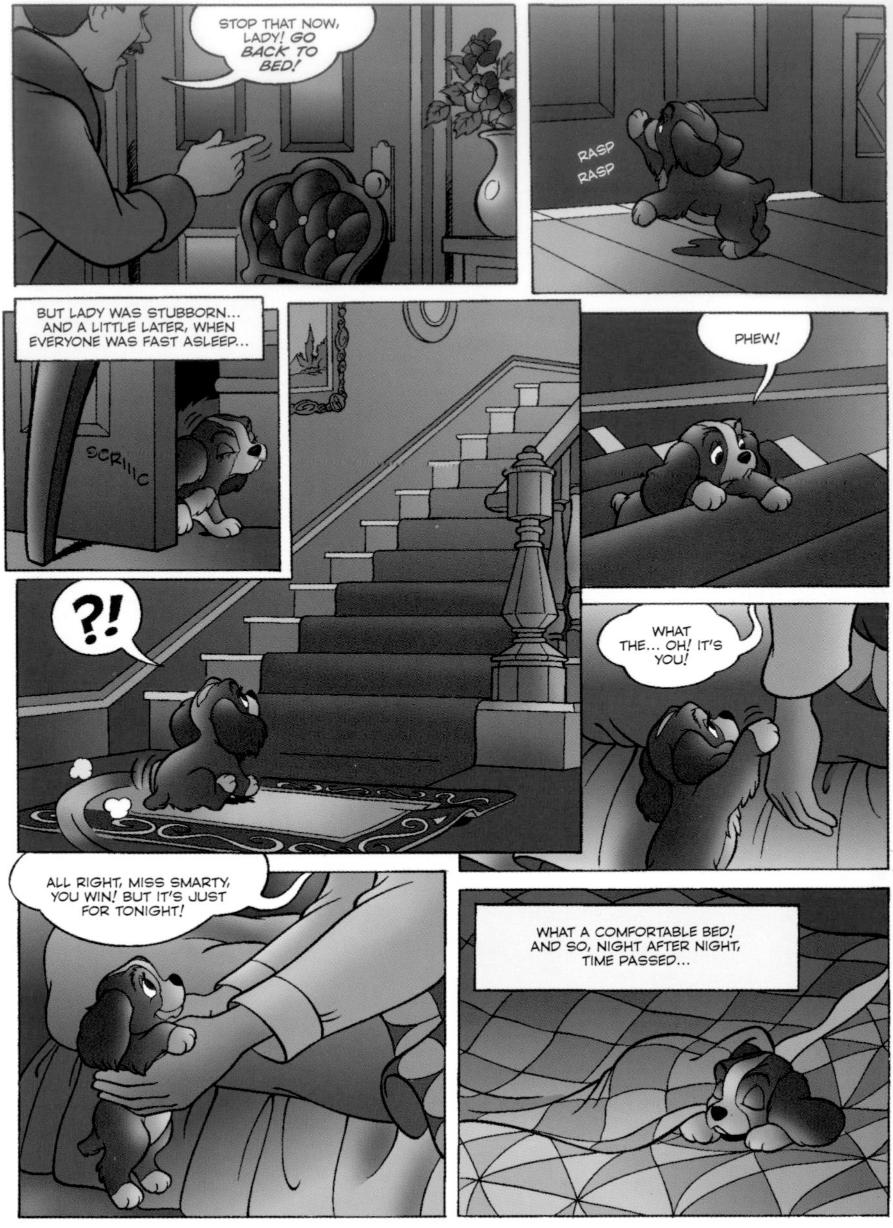
STOP THAT NOW, LADY! GO BACK TO BED!
RASP RASP
BUT LADY WAS STUBBORN... AND A LITTLE LATER, WHEN EVERYONE WAS FAST ASLEEP...
SCRIIIC
PHEW!
?!
WHAT THE... OH! IT'S YOU!
ALL RIGHT, MISS SMARTY, YOU WIN! BUT IT'S JUST FOR TONIGHT!
WHAT A COMFORTABLE BED! AND SO, NIGHT AFTER NIGHT, TIME PASSED...

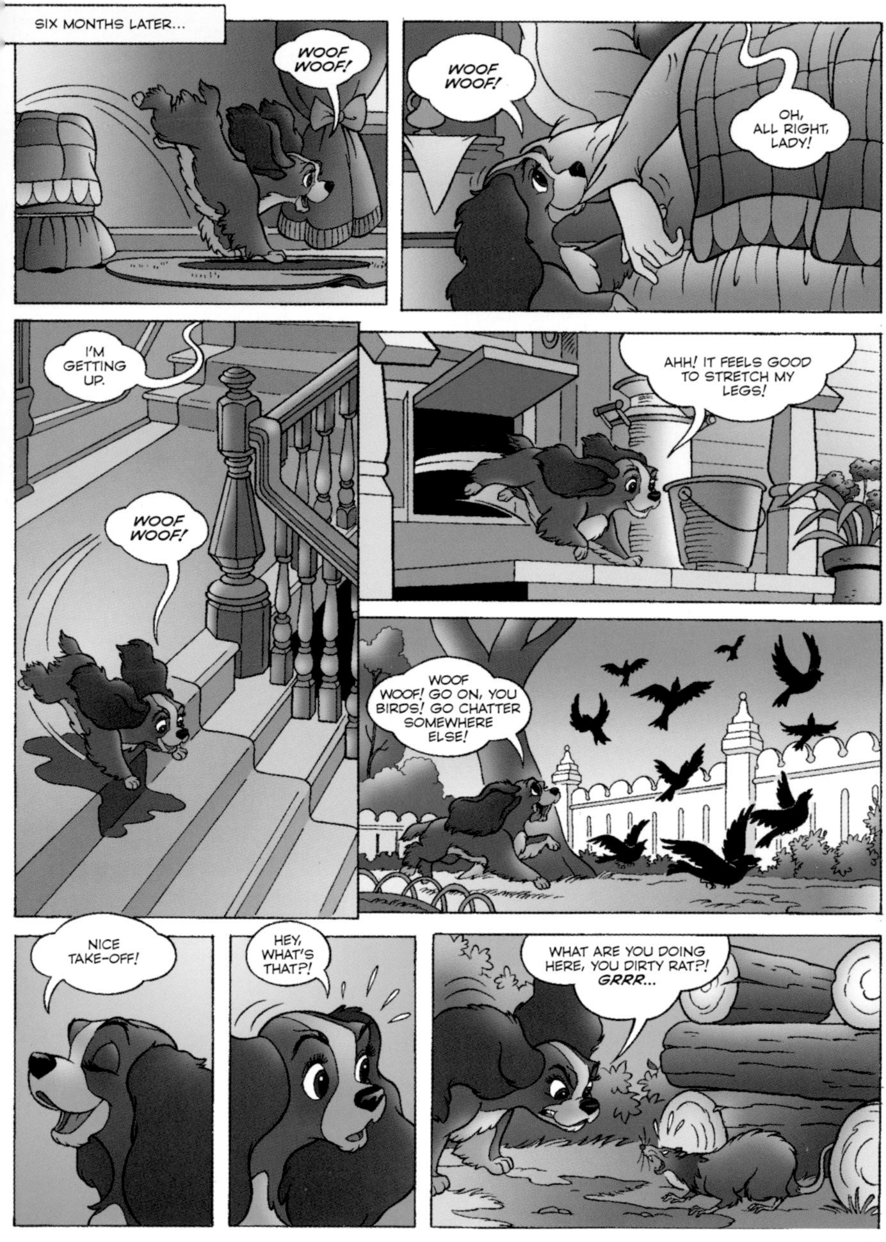

SIX MONTHS LATER...
WOOF WOOF!
WOOF WOOF!
OH, ALL RIGHT, LADY!
I'M GETTING UP.
WOOF WOOF!
AHH! IT FEELS GOOD TO STRETCH MY LEGS!
WOOF WOOF! GO ON, YOU BIRDS! GO CHATTER SOMEWHERE ELSE!
NICE TAKE-OFF!
HEY, WHAT'S THAT?!
WHAT ARE YOU DOING HERE, YOU DIRTY RAT?! GRRR...

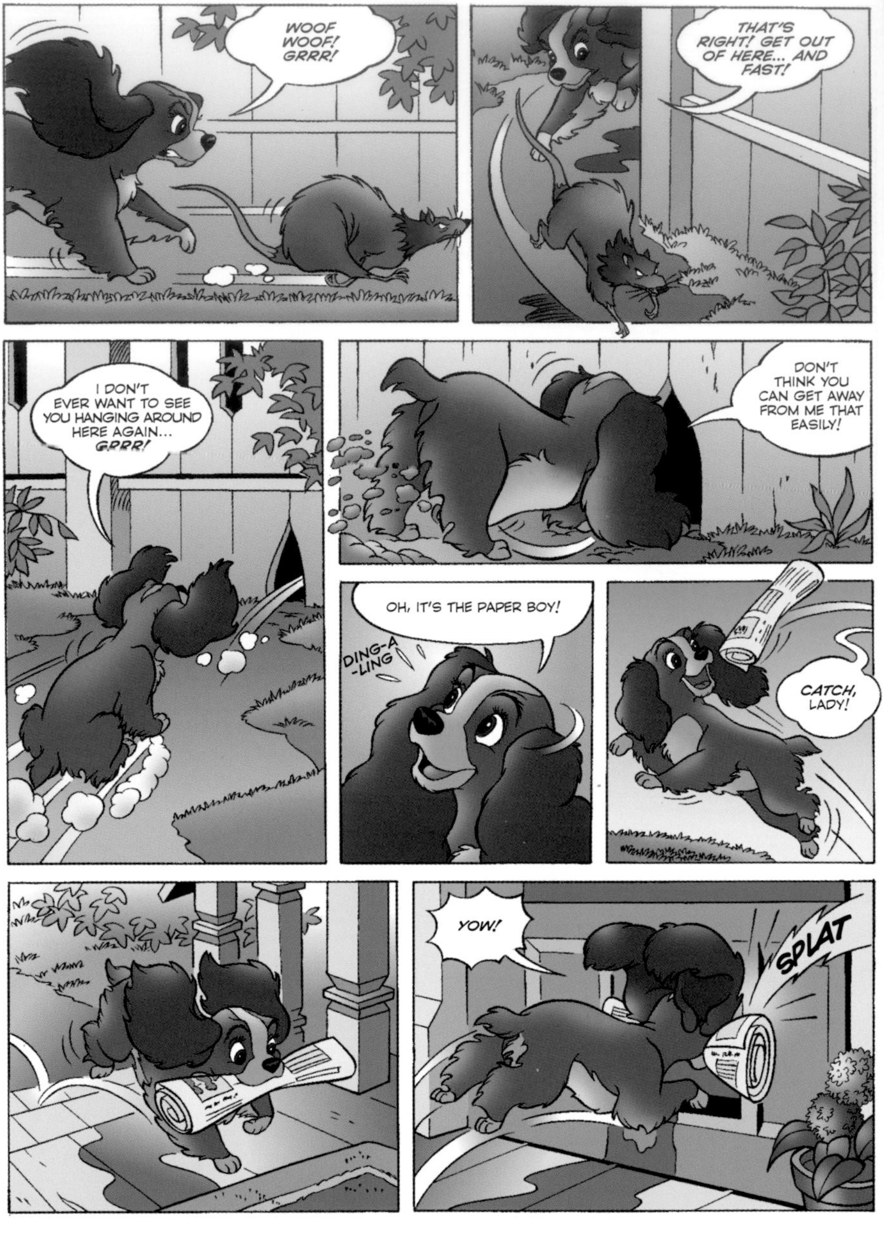

WOOF WOOF! GRRR!
THAT'S RIGHT! GET OUT OF HERE... AND FAST!
I DON'T EVER WANT TO SEE YOU HANGING AROUND HERE AGAIN... GRRR!
DON'T THINK YOU CAN GET AWAY FROM ME THAT EASILY!
OH, IT'S THE PAPER BOY!
DING-A-LING
CATCH, LADY!
YOW!
SPLAT

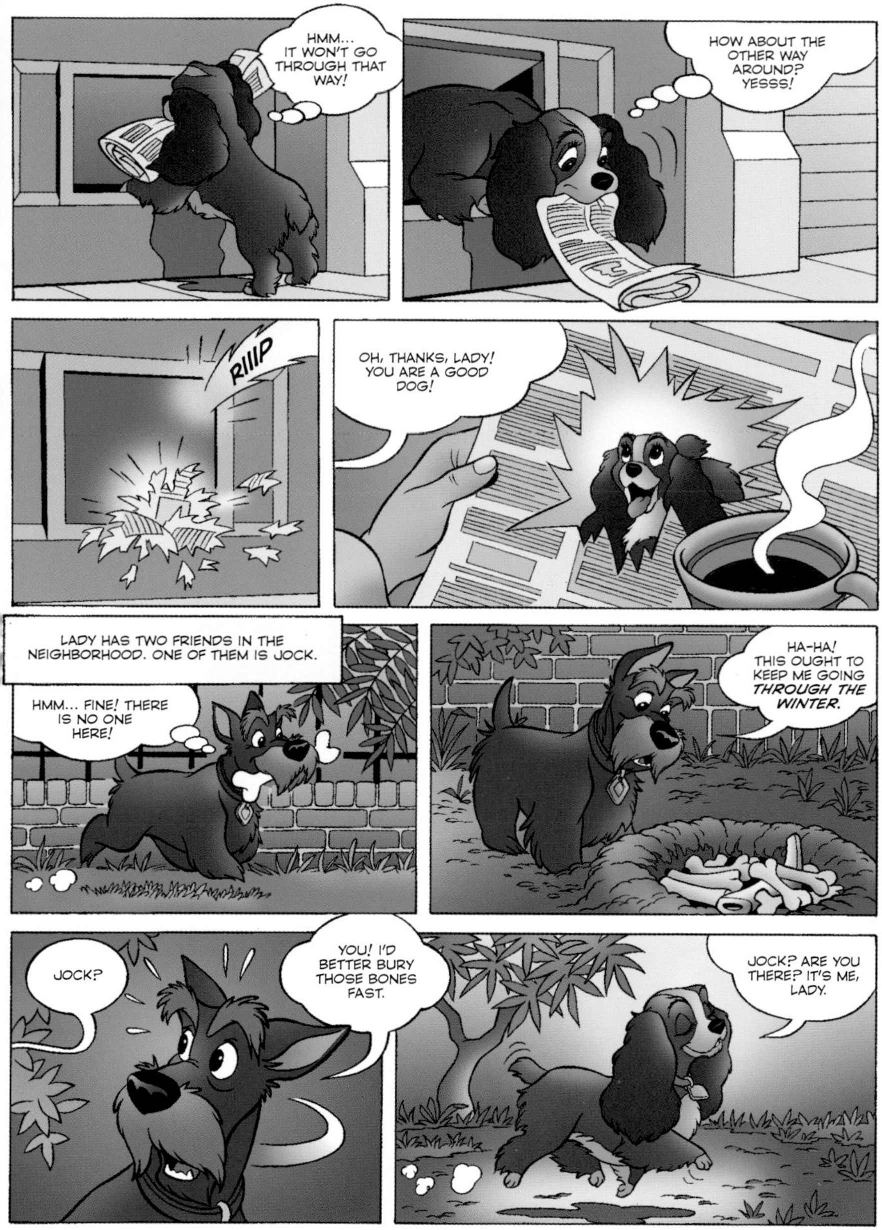
HMM... IT WON'T GO THROUGH THAT WAY!
HOW ABOUT THE OTHER WAY AROUND? YESSS!
RIIIP
OH, THANKS, LADY! YOU ARE A GOOD DOG!
LADY HAS TWO FRIENDS IN THE NEIGHBORHOOD. ONE OF THEM IS JOCK.
HMM... FINE! THERE IS NO ONE HERE!
HA-HA! THIS OUGHT TO KEEP ME GOING THROUGH THE WINTER.
JOCK?
YOU! I'D BETTER BURY THOSE BONES FAST.
JOCK? ARE YOU THERE? IT'S ME, LADY.

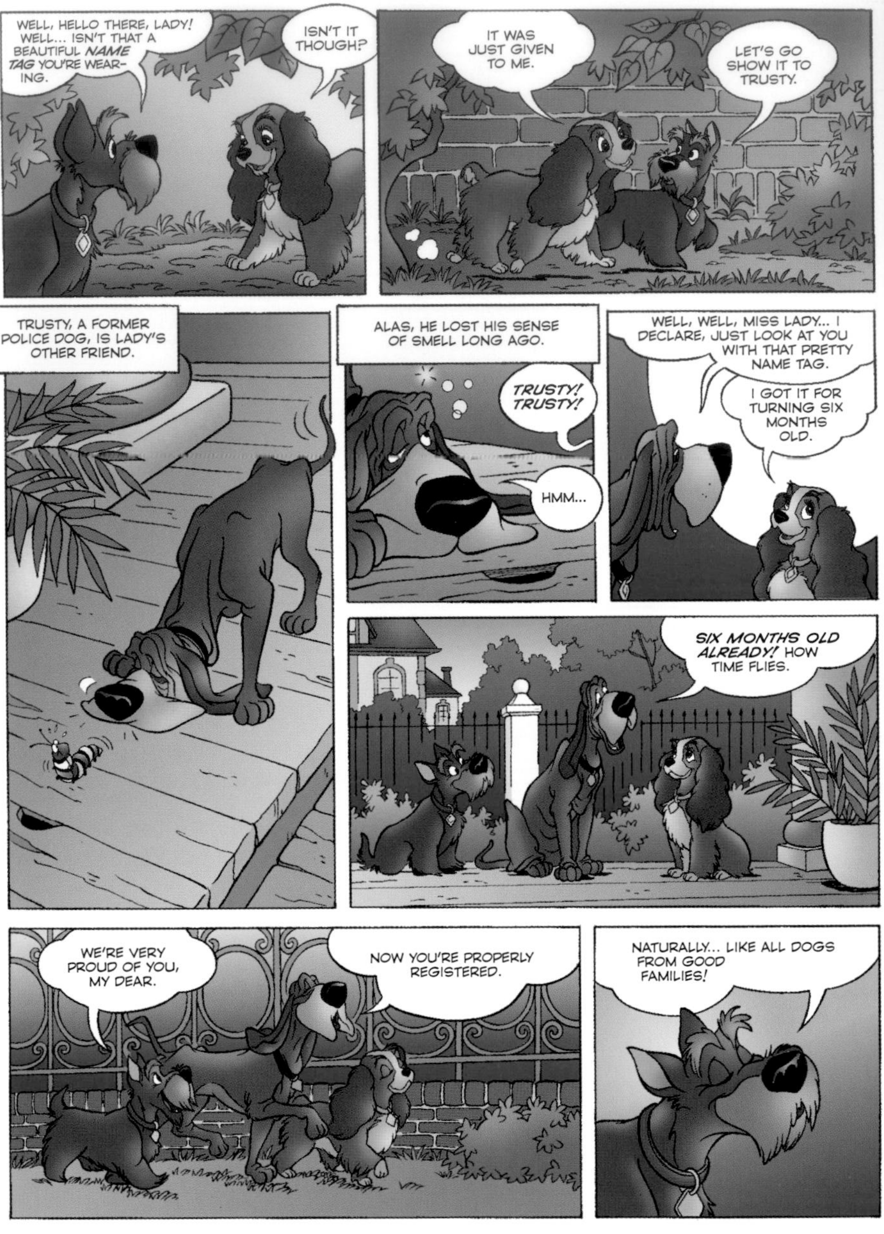
WELL, HELLO THERE, LADY! WELL... ISN'T THAT A BEAUTIFUL NAME TAG YOU'RE WEAR-ING.
ISN'T IT THOUGH?
IT WAS JUST GIVEN TO ME.
LET'S GO SHOW IT TO TRUSTY.
TRUSTY, A FORMER POLICE DOG, IS LADY'S OTHER FRIEND.
ALAS, HE LOST HIS SENSE OF SMELL LONG AGO.
TRUSTY! TRUSTY!
HMM...
WELL, WELL, MISS LADY... I DECLARE, JUST LOOK AT YOU WITH THAT PRETTY NAME TAG.
I GOT IT FOR TURNING SIX MONTHS OLD.
SIX MONTHS OLD ALREADY! HOW TIME FLIES.
WE'RE VERY PROUD OF YOU, MY DEAR.
NOW YOU'RE PROPERLY REGISTERED.
NATURALLY... LIKE ALL DOGS FROM GOOD FAMILIES!

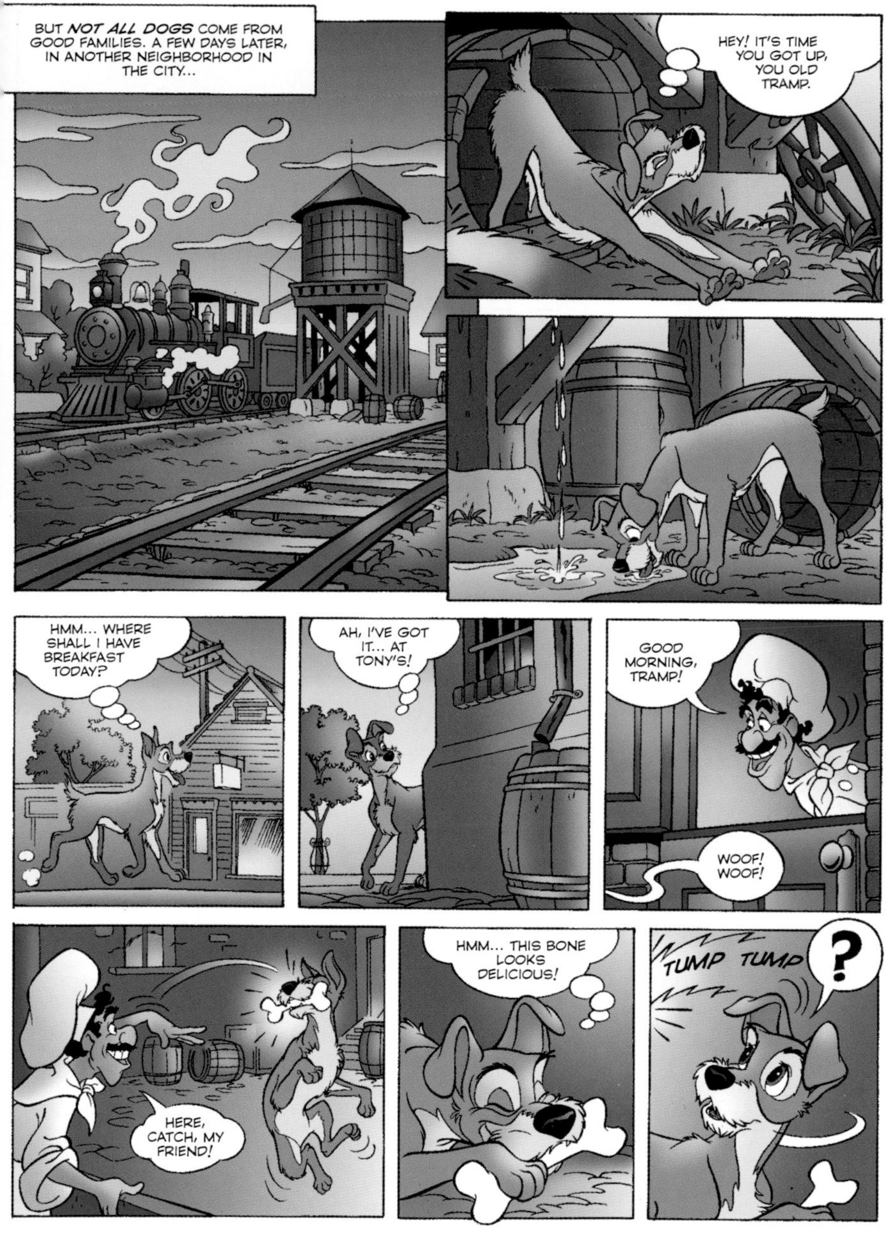

BUT NOT ALL DOGS COME FROM GOOD FAMILIES. A FEW DAYS LATER, IN ANOTHER NEIGHBORHOOD IN THE CITY...
HEY! IT'S TIME YOU GOT UP, YOU OLD TRAMP.
HMM... WHERE SHALL I HAVE BREAKFAST TODAY?
AH, I'VE GOT IT... AT TONY'S!
GOOD MORNING, TRAMP!
WOOF! WOOF!
HERE, CATCH, MY FRIEND!
HMM... THIS BONE LOOKS DELICIOUS!
TUMP TUMP
?

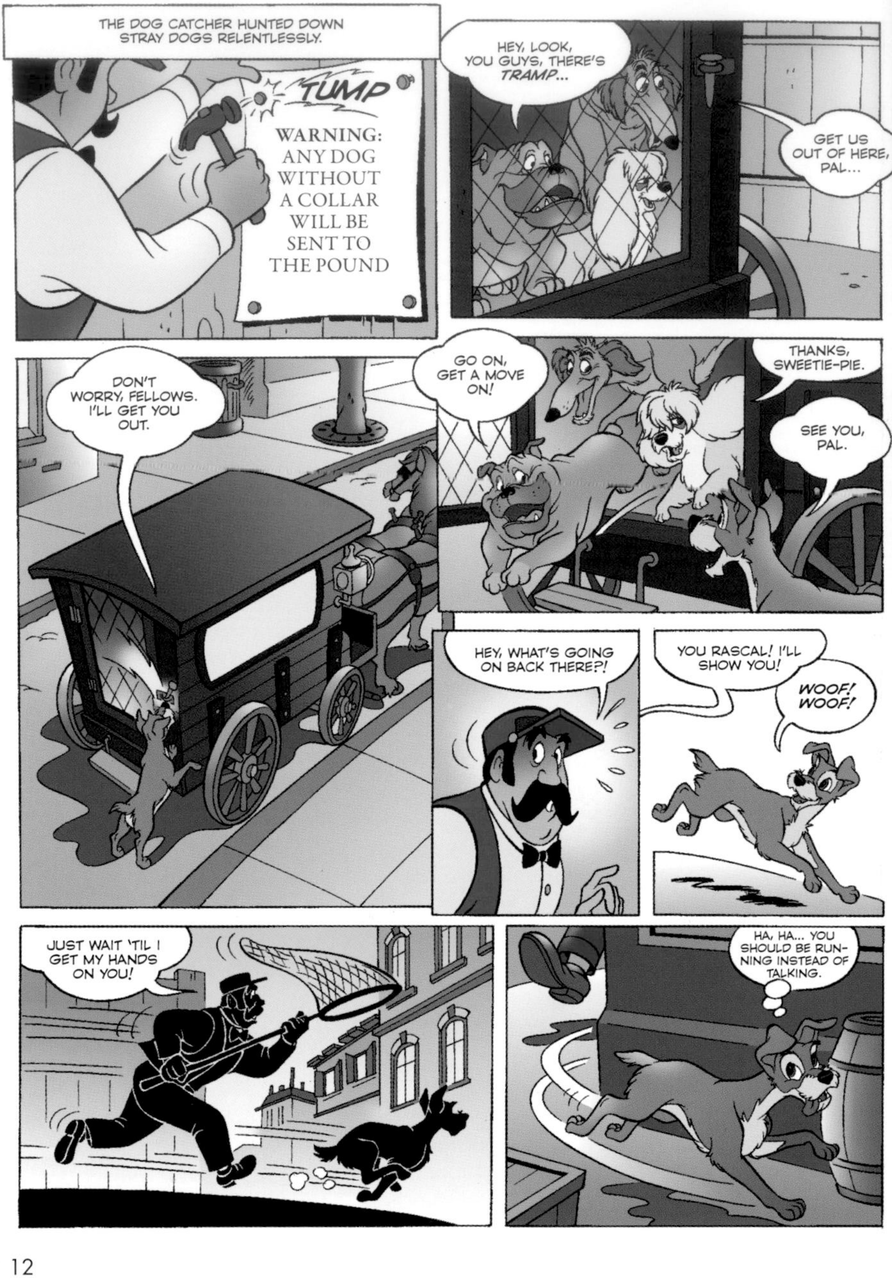

THE DOG CATCHER HUNTED DOWN STRAY DOGS RELENTLESSLY.
TUMP
WARNING: ANY DOG WITHOUT A COLLAR WILL BE SENT TO THE POUND
HEY, LOOK, YOU GUYS, THERE'S TRAMP...
GET US OUT OF HERE, PAL...
DON'T WORRY, FELLOWS. I'LL GET YOU OUT.
GO ON, GET A MOVE ON!
THANKS, SWEETIE-PIE.
SEE YOU, PAL.
HEY, WHAT'S GOING ON BACK THERE?!
YOU RASCAL! I'LL SHOW YOU!
WOOF! WOOF!
JUST WAIT 'TIL I GET MY HANDS ON YOU!
HA, HA... YOU SHOULD BE RUNNING INSTEAD OF TALKING.

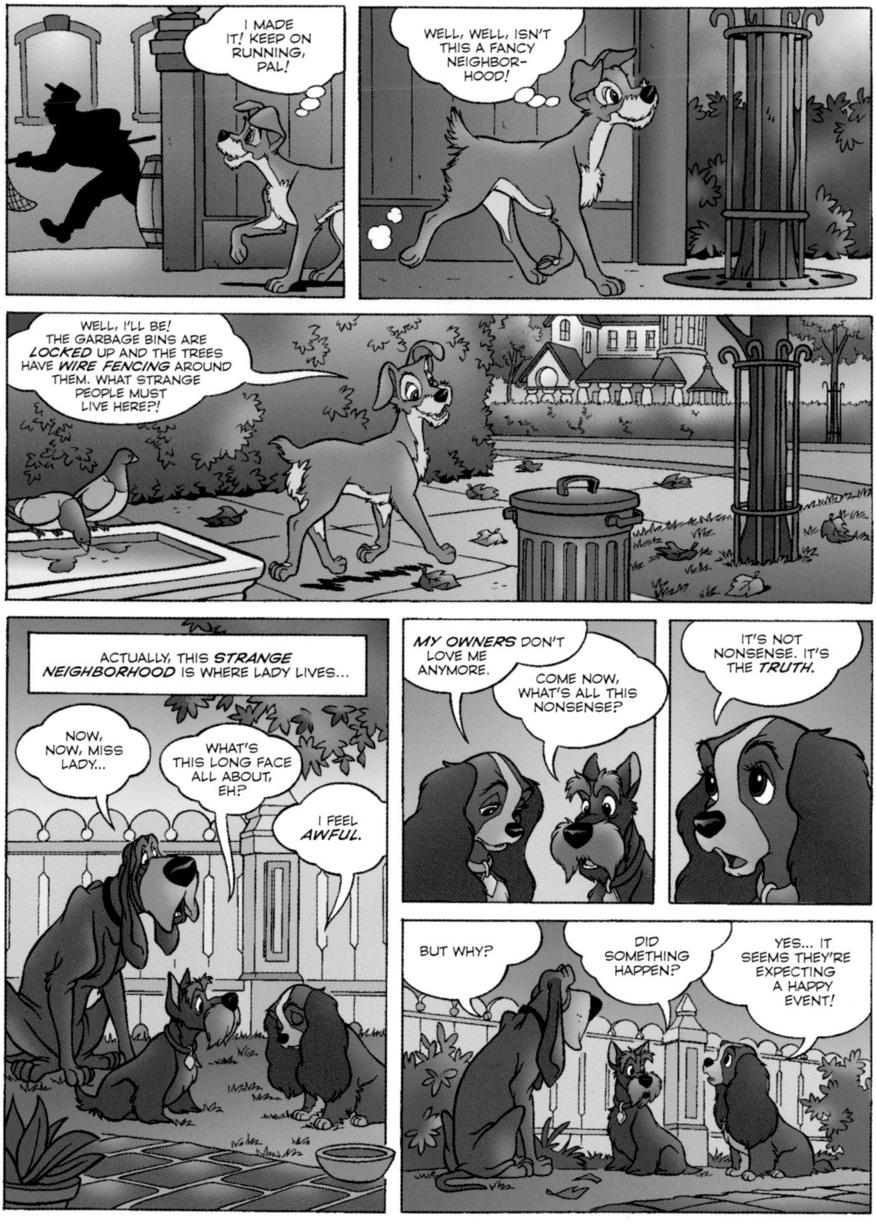

I MADE IT! KEEP ON RUNNING, PAL!
WELL, WELL, ISN'T THIS A FANCY NEIGHBOR-HOOD!
WELL, I'LL BE! THE GARBAGE BINS ARE LOCKED UP AND THE TREES HAVE WIRE FENCING AROUND THEM. WHAT STRANGE PEOPLE MUST LIVE HERE?!
ACTUALLY, THIS STRANGE NEIGHBORHOOD IS WHERE LADY LIVES...
NOW, NOW, MISS LADY...
WHAT'S THIS LONG FACE ALL ABOUT, EH?
I FEEL AWFUL.
MY OWNERS DON'T LOVE ME ANYMORE.
COME NOW, WHAT'S ALL THIS NONSENSE?
IT'S NOT NONSENSE. IT'S THE TRUTH.
BUT WHY?
DID SOMETHING HAPPEN?
YES... IT SEEMS THEY'RE EXPECTING A HAPPY EVENT!

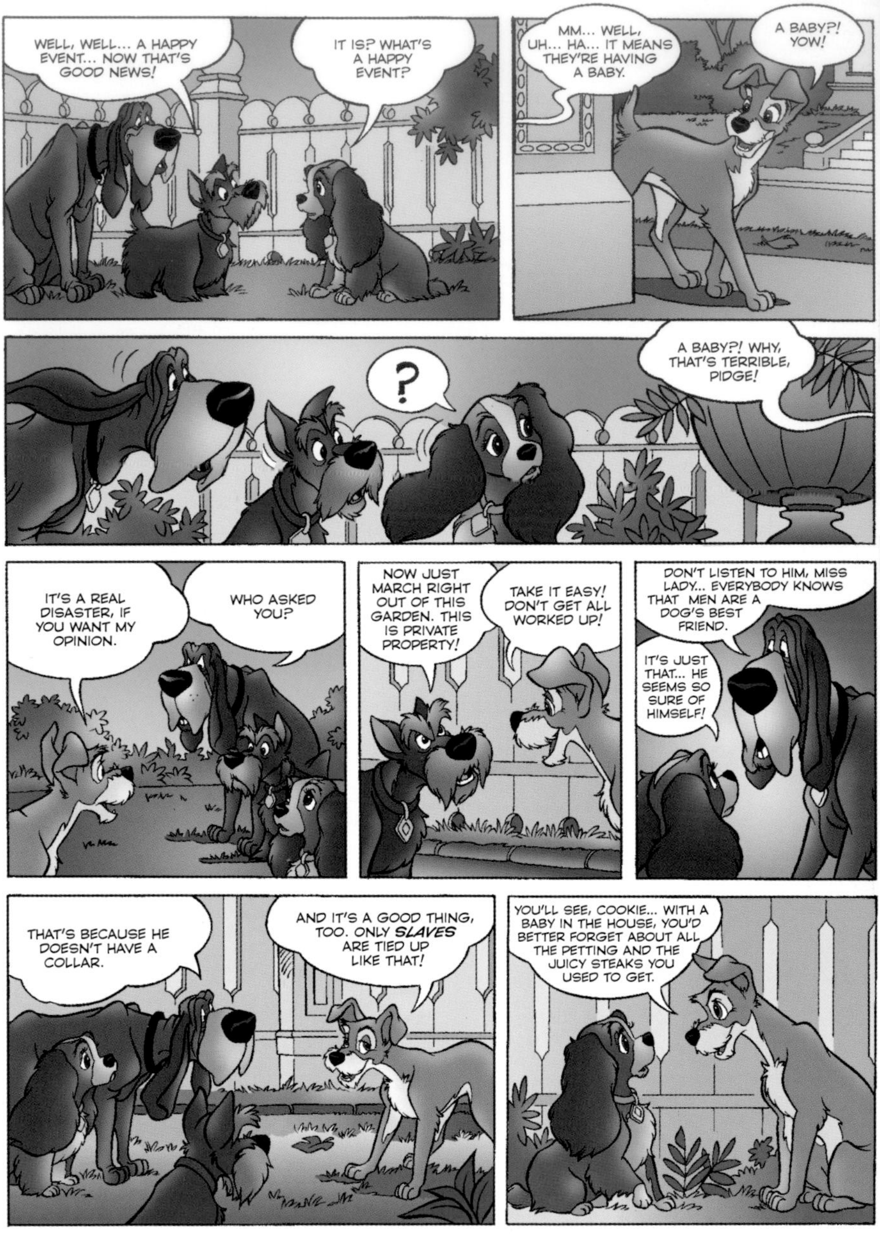

WELL, WELL... A HAPPY EVENT... NOW THAT'S GOOD NEWS!
IT IS? WHAT'S A HAPPY EVENT?
MM... WELL, UH... HA... IT MEANS THEY'RE HAVING A BABY.
A BABY?! YOW!
?
A BABY?! WHY, THAT'S TERRIBLE, PIDGE!
IT'S A REAL DISASTER, IF YOU WANT MY OPINION.
WHO ASKED YOU?
NOW JUST MARCH RIGHT OUT OF THIS GARDEN. THIS IS PRIVATE PROPERTY!
TAKE IT EASY! DON'T GET ALL WORKED UP!
DON'T LISTEN TO HIM, MISS LADY... EVERYBODY KNOWS THAT MEN ARE A DOG'S BEST FRIEND.
IT'S JUST THAT... HE SEEMS SO SURE OF HIMSELF!
THAT'S BECAUSE HE DOESN'T HAVE A COLLAR.
AND IT'S A GOOD THING, TOO. ONLY SLAVES ARE TIED UP LIKE THAT!
YOU'LL SEE, COOKIE... WITH A BABY IN THE HOUSE, YOU'D BETTER FORGET ABOUT ALL THE PETTING AND THE JUICY STEAKS YOU USED TO GET.

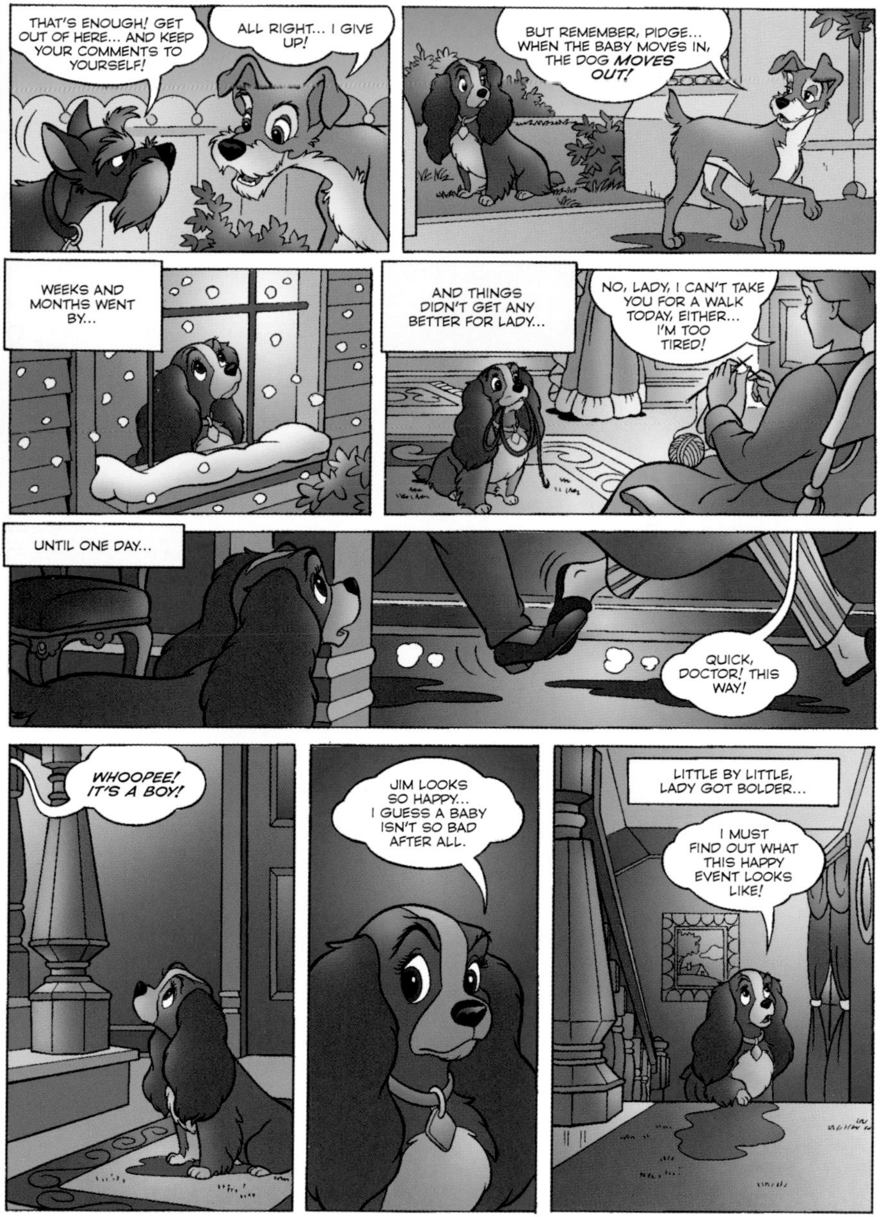
THAT'S ENOUGH! GET OUT OF HERE... AND KEEP YOUR COMMENTS TO YOURSELF!
ALL RIGHT... I GIVE UP!
BUT REMEMBER, PIDGE... WHEN THE BABY MOVES IN, THE DOG MOVES OUT!
WEEKS AND MONTHS WENT BY...
AND THINGS DIDN'T GET ANY BETTER FOR LADY...
NO, LADY, I CAN'T TAKE YOU FOR A WALK TODAY, EITHER... I'M TOO TIRED!
UNTIL ONE DAY...
QUICK, DOCTOR! THIS WAY!
WHOOPEE! IT'S A BOY!
JIM LOOKS SO HAPPY... I GUESS A BABY ISN'T SO BAD AFTER ALL.
LITTLE BY LITTLE, LADY GOT BOLDER...
I MUST FIND OUT WHAT THIS HAPPY EVENT LOOKS LIKE!

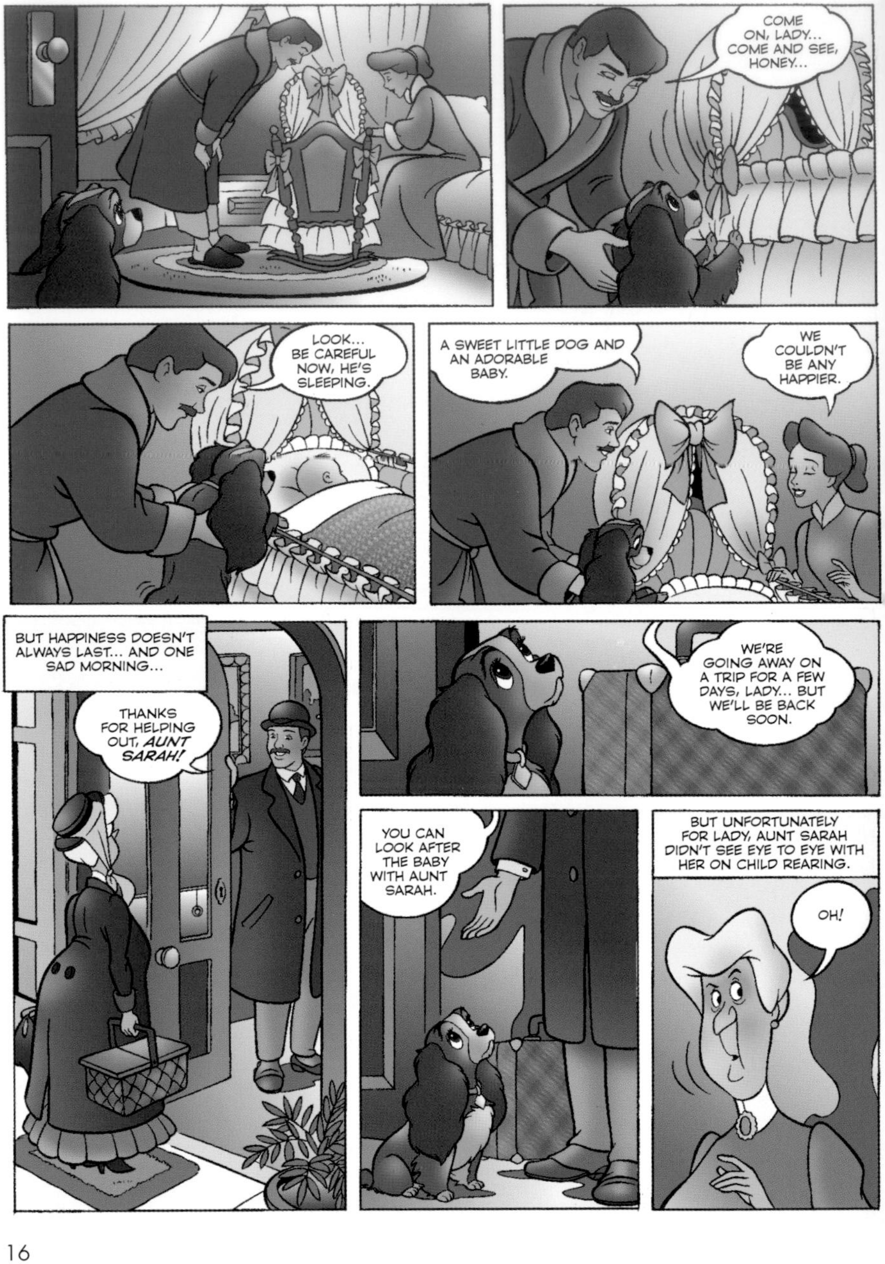
COME ON, LADY... COME AND SEE, HONEY...
LOOK... BE CAREFUL NOW, HE'S SLEEPING.
A SWEET LITTLE DOG AND AN ADORABLE BABY.
WE COULDN'T BE ANY HAPPIER.
BUT HAPPINESS DOESN'T ALWAYS LAST... AND ONE SAD MORNING...
THANKS FOR HELPING OUT, AUNT SARAH!
WE'RE GOING AWAY ON A TRIP FOR A FEW DAYS, LADY... BUT WE'LL BE BACK SOON.
YOU CAN LOOK AFTER THE BABY WITH AUNT SARAH.
BUT UNFORTUNATELY FOR LADY, AUNT SARAH DIDN'T SEE EYE TO EYE WITH HER ON CHILD REARING.
OH!

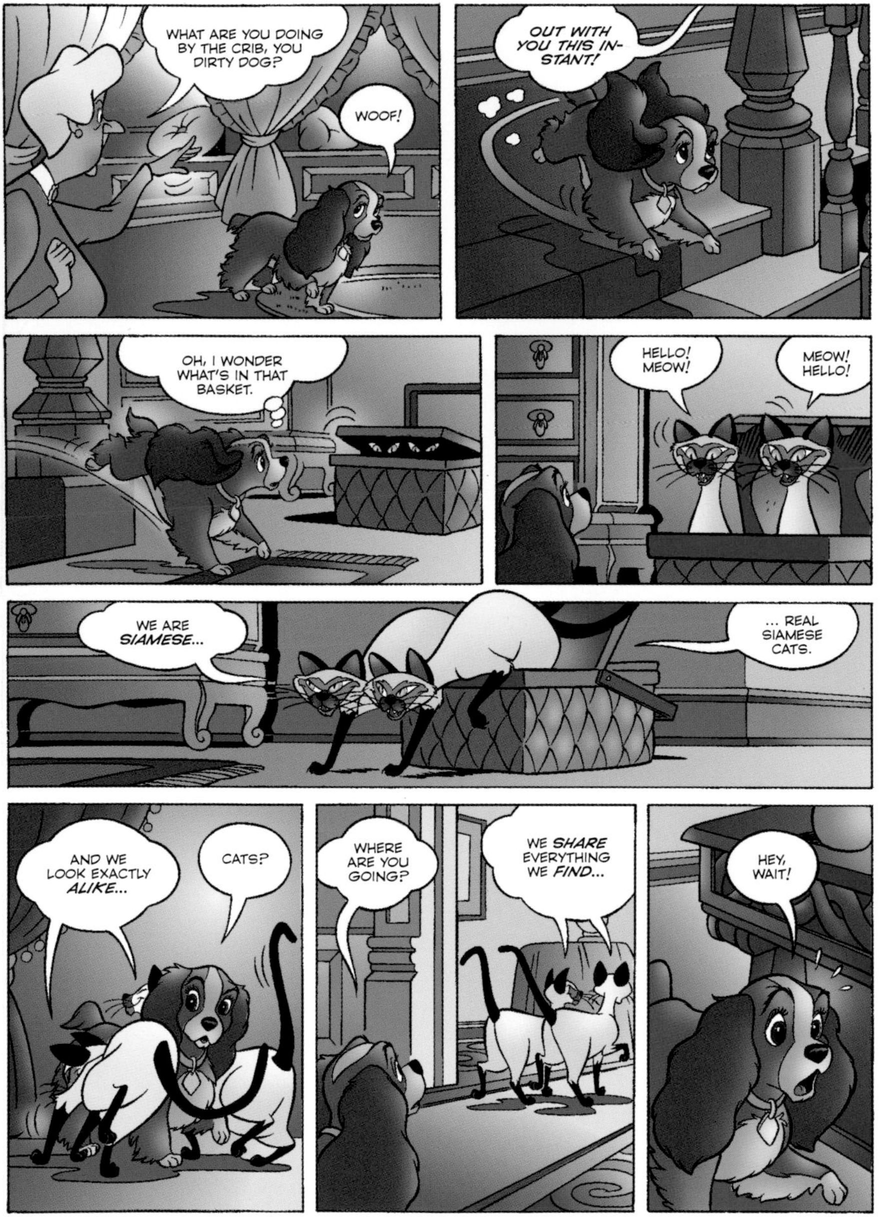
WHAT ARE YOU DOING BY THE CRIB, YOU DIRTY DOG?
WOOF!
OUT WITH YOU THIS IN-STANT!
OH, I WONDER WHAT'S IN THAT BASKET.
HELLO! MEOW!
MEOW! HELLO!
WE ARE SIAMESE...
... REAL SIAMESE CATS.
AND WE LOOK EXACTLY ALIKE...
CATS?
WHERE ARE YOU GOING?
WE SHARE EVERYTHING WE FIND...
HEY, WAIT!

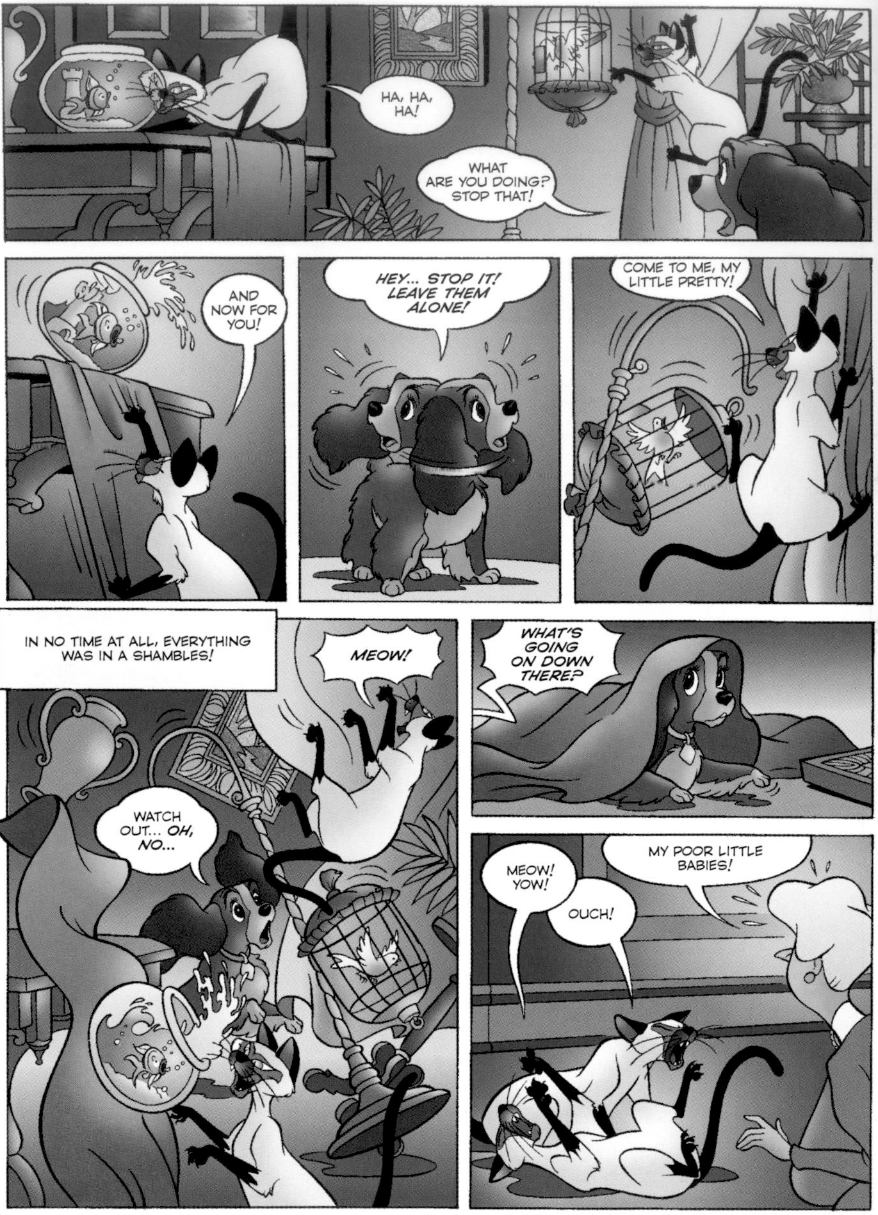
HA, HA, HA!
WHAT ARE YOU DOING? STOP THAT!
AND NOW FOR YOU!
HEY... STOP IT! LEAVE THEM ALONE!
COME TO ME, MY LITTLE PRETTY!
IN NO TIME AT ALL, EVERYTHING WAS IN A SHAMBLES!
MEOW!
WATCH OUT... OH, NO...
WHAT'S GOING ON DOWN THERE?
MEOW! YOW!
OUCH!
MY POOR LITTLE BABIES!

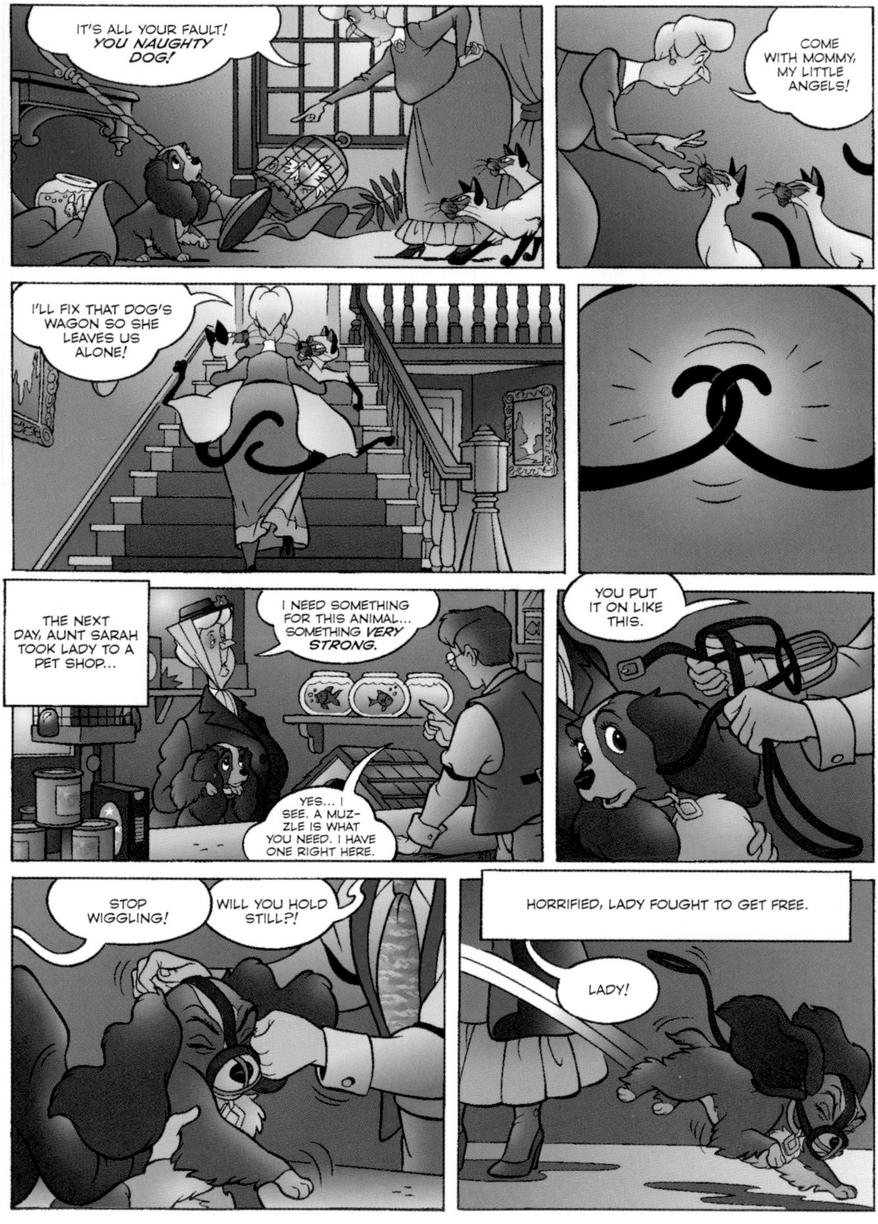
IT'S ALL YOUR FAULT! ***YOU NAUGHTY DOG!***
COME WITH MOMMY, MY LITTLE ANGELS!
I'LL FIX THAT DOG'S WAGON SO SHE LEAVES US ALONE!
THE NEXT DAY, AUNT SARAH TOOK LADY TO A PET SHOP...
I NEED SOMETHING FOR THIS ANIMAL... SOMETHING ***VERY STRONG.***
YES... I SEE. A MUZ-ZLE IS WHAT YOU NEED. I HAVE ONE RIGHT HERE.
YOU PUT IT ON LIKE THIS.
STOP WIGGLING!
WILL YOU HOLD STILL?!
HORRIFIED, LADY FOUGHT TO GET FREE.
LADY!

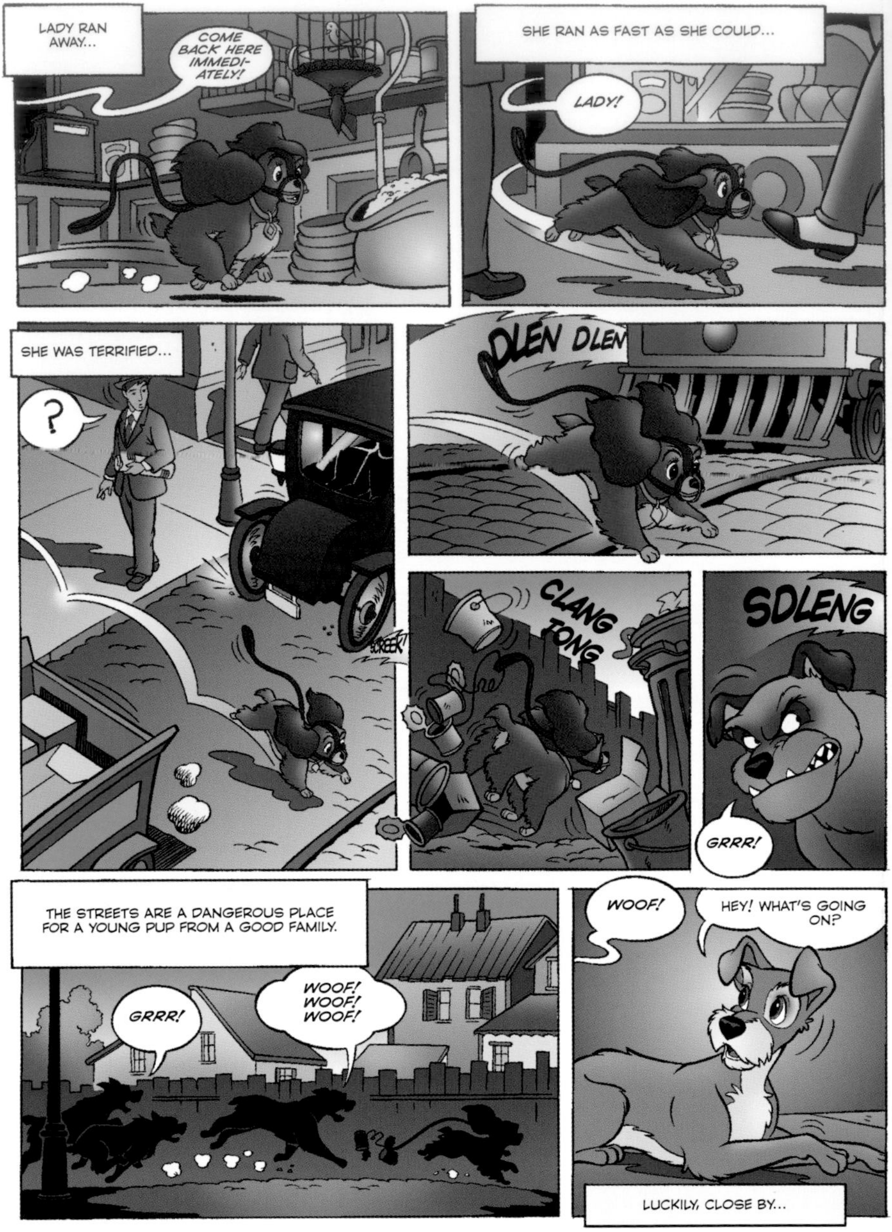
LADY RAN AWAY...
COME BACK HERE IMMEDIATELY!
SHE RAN AS FAST AS SHE COULD...
LADY!
SHE WAS TERRIFIED...
?
SCREECH!
DLEN DLEN
CLANG TONG
SDLENG
GRRR!
THE STREETS ARE A DANGEROUS PLACE FOR A YOUNG PUP FROM A GOOD FAMILY.
GRRR!
WOOF! WOOF! WOOF!
WOOF!
HEY! WHAT'S GOING ON?
LUCKILY, CLOSE BY...

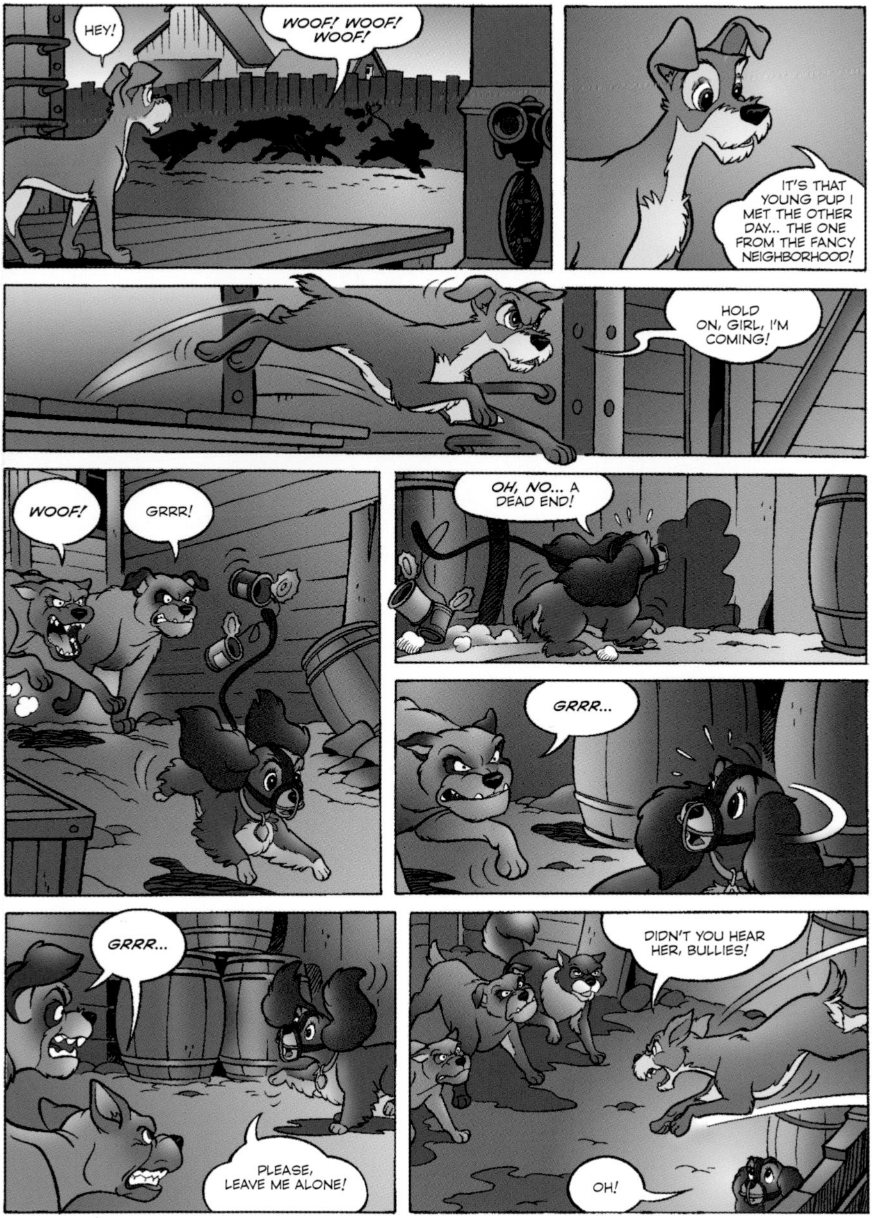

HEY!
WOOF! WOOF! WOOF!
IT'S THAT YOUNG PUP I MET THE OTHER DAY... THE ONE FROM THE FANCY NEIGHBORHOOD!
HOLD ON, GIRL, I'M COMING!
WOOF!
GRRR!
OH, NO... A DEAD END!
GRRR...
GRRR...
PLEASE, LEAVE ME ALONE!
DIDN'T YOU HEAR HER, BULLIES!
OH!

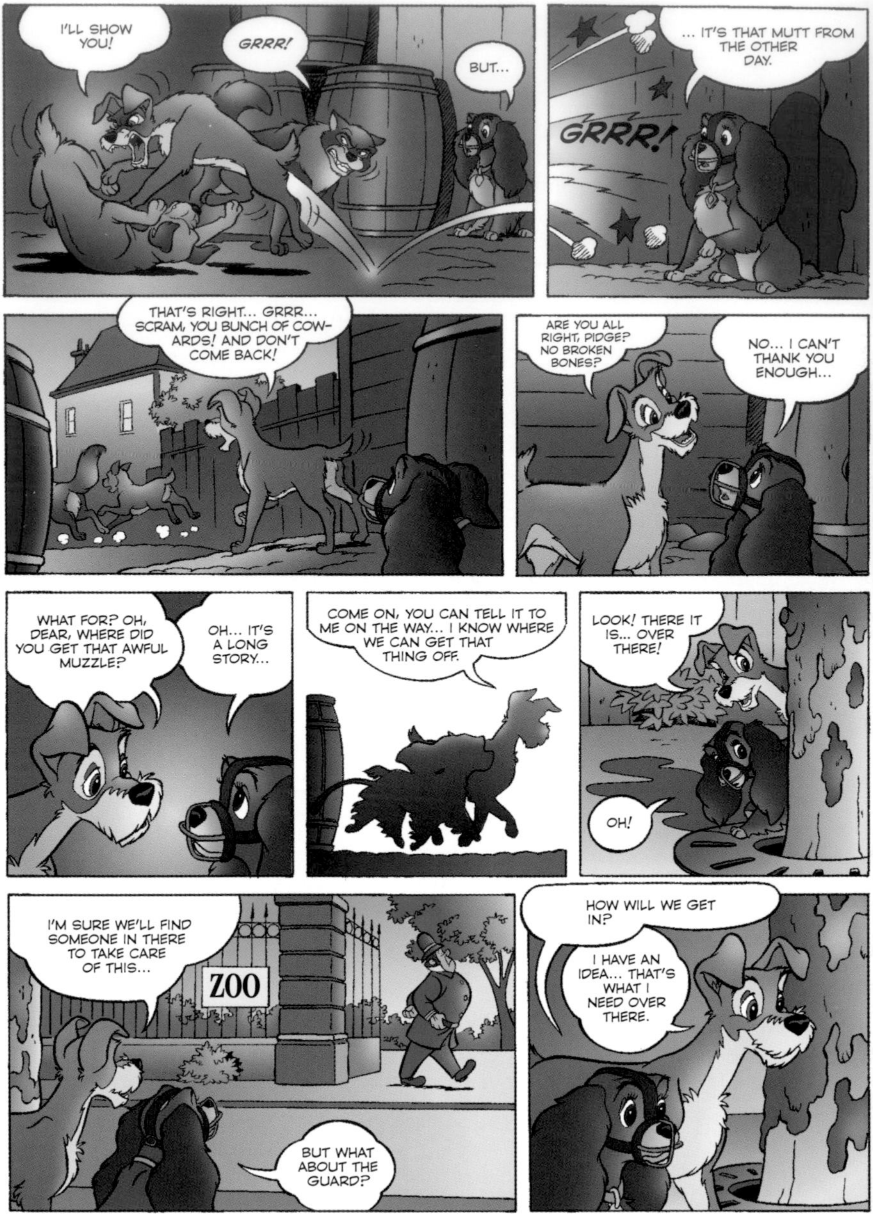

I'LL SHOW YOU!
GRRR!
BUT...
... IT'S THAT MUTT FROM THE OTHER DAY.
GRRR!
THAT'S RIGHT... GRRR... SCRAM, YOU BUNCH OF COW-ARDS! AND DON'T COME BACK!
ARE YOU ALL RIGHT, PIDGE? NO BROKEN BONES?
NO... I CAN'T THANK YOU ENOUGH...
WHAT FOR? OH, DEAR, WHERE DID YOU GET THAT AWFUL MUZZLE?
OH... IT'S A LONG STORY...
COME ON, YOU CAN TELL IT TO ME ON THE WAY... I KNOW WHERE WE CAN GET THAT THING OFF.
LOOK! THERE IT IS... OVER THERE!
OH!
I'M SURE WE'LL FIND SOMEONE IN THERE TO TAKE CARE OF THIS...
ZOO
BUT WHAT ABOUT THE GUARD?
HOW WILL WE GET IN?
I HAVE AN IDEA... THAT'S WHAT I NEED OVER THERE.

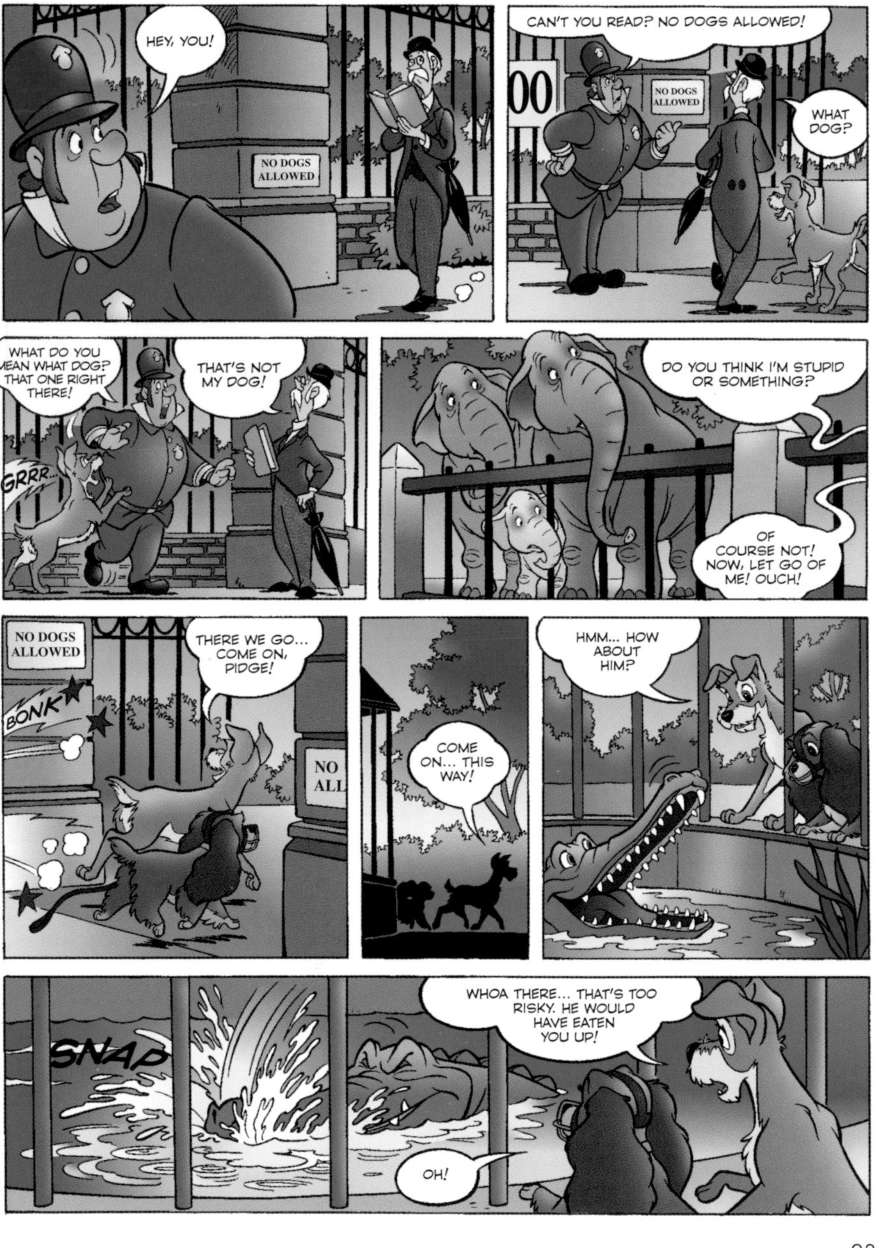

HEY, YOU!
NO DOGS ALLOWED
CAN'T YOU READ? NO DOGS ALLOWED!
NO DOGS ALLOWED
WHAT DOG?
WHAT DO YOU MEAN WHAT DOG? THAT ONE RIGHT THERE!
THAT'S NOT MY DOG!
GRRR...
DO YOU THINK I'M STUPID OR SOMETHING?
OF COURSE NOT! NOW, LET GO OF ME! OUCH!
NO DOGS ALLOWED
THERE WE GO... COME ON, PIDGE!
BONK
COME ON... THIS WAY!
HMM... HOW ABOUT HIM?
SNAP
WHOA THERE... THAT'S TOO RISKY. HE WOULD HAVE EATEN YOU UP!
OH!

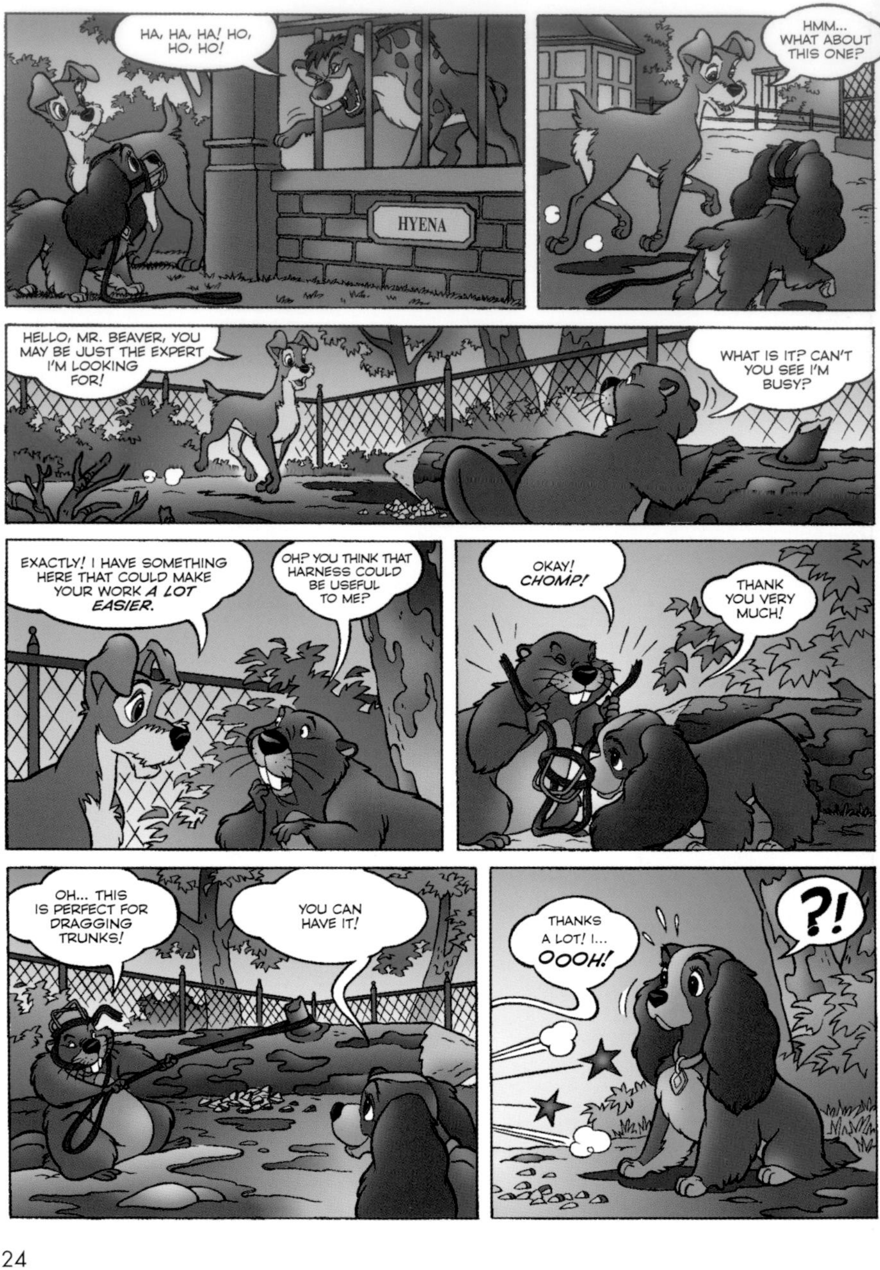
HA, HA, HA! HO, HO, HO!
HYENA
HMM... WHAT ABOUT THIS ONE?
HELLO, MR. BEAVER, YOU MAY BE JUST THE EXPERT I'M LOOKING FOR!
WHAT IS IT? CAN'T YOU SEE I'M BUSY?
EXACTLY! I HAVE SOMETHING HERE THAT COULD MAKE YOUR WORK A LOT EASIER.
OH? YOU THINK THAT HARNESS COULD BE USEFUL TO ME?
OKAY! CHOMP!
THANK YOU VERY MUCH!
OH... THIS IS PERFECT FOR DRAGGING TRUNKS!
YOU CAN HAVE IT!
THANKS A LOT! I... OOOH!
?!

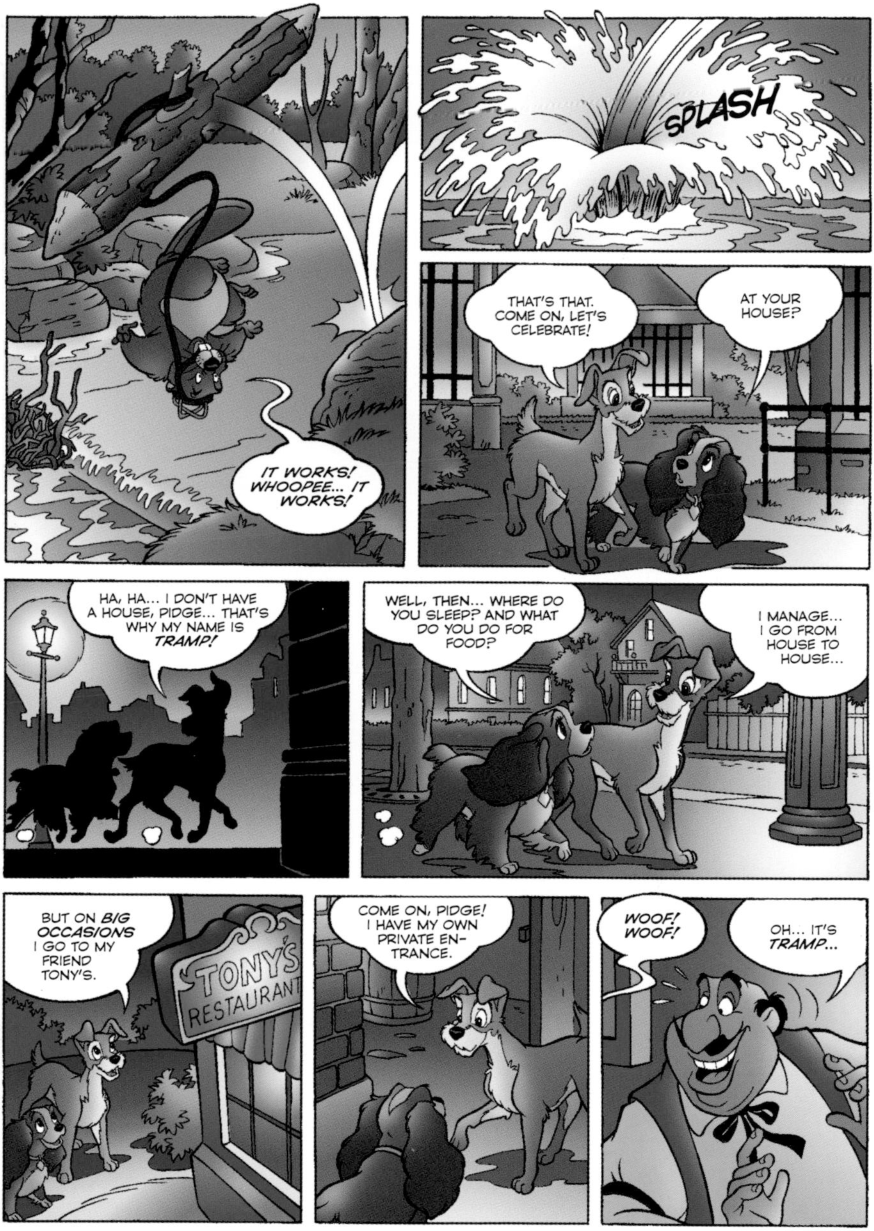
IT WORKS! WHOOPEE... IT WORKS!
SPLASH
THAT'S THAT. COME ON, LET'S CELEBRATE!
AT YOUR HOUSE?
HA, HA... I DON'T HAVE A HOUSE, PIDGE... THAT'S WHY MY NAME IS TRAMP!
WELL, THEN... WHERE DO YOU SLEEP? AND WHAT DO YOU DO FOR FOOD?
I MANAGE... I GO FROM HOUSE TO HOUSE...
BUT ON BIG OCCASIONS I GO TO MY FRIEND TONY'S.
TONY'S RESTAURANT
COME ON, PIDGE! I HAVE MY OWN PRIVATE EN-TRANCE.
WOOF! WOOF!
OH... IT'S TRAMP...

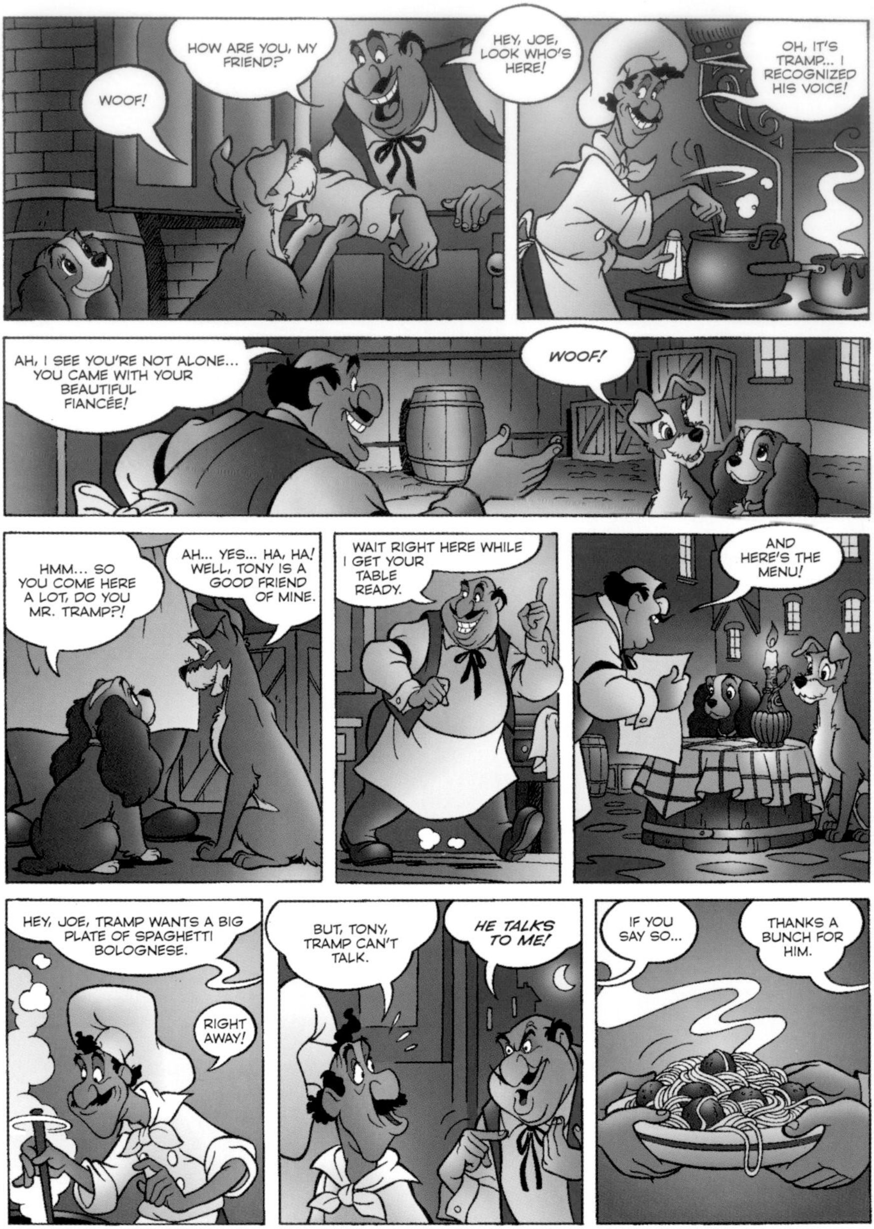
WOOF!
HOW ARE YOU, MY FRIEND?
HEY, JOE, LOOK WHO'S HERE!
OH, IT'S TRAMP... I RECOGNIZED HIS VOICE!
AH, I SEE YOU'RE NOT ALONE... YOU CAME WITH YOUR BEAUTIFUL FIANCÉE!
WOOF!
HMM... SO YOU COME HERE A LOT, DO YOU MR. TRAMP?!
AH... YES... HA, HA! WELL, TONY IS A GOOD FRIEND OF MINE.
WAIT RIGHT HERE WHILE I GET YOUR TABLE READY.
AND HERE'S THE MENU!
HEY, JOE, TRAMP WANTS A BIG PLATE OF SPAGHETTI BOLOGNESE.
RIGHT AWAY!
BUT, TONY, TRAMP CAN'T TALK.
HE TALKS TO ME!
IF YOU SAY SO...
THANKS A BUNCH FOR HIM.

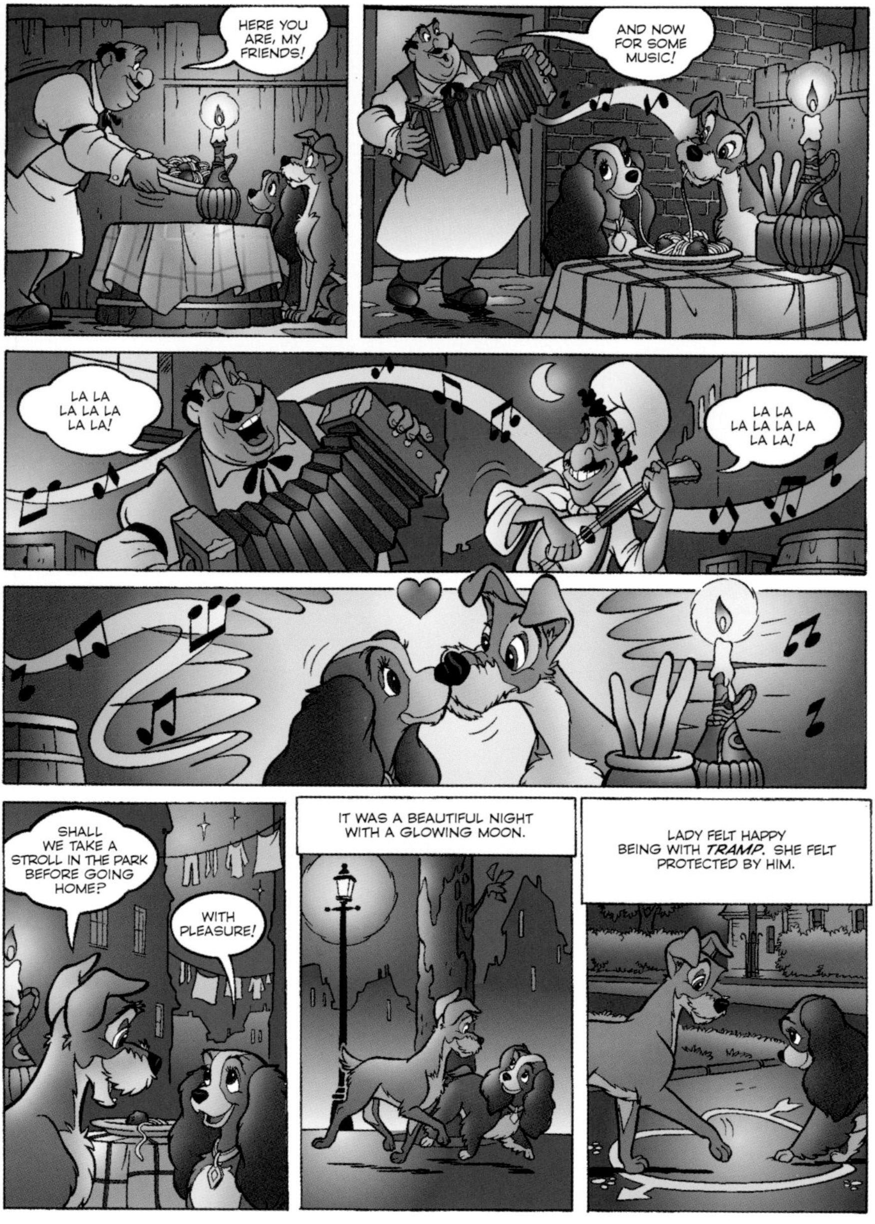
HERE YOU ARE, MY FRIENDS!
AND NOW FOR SOME MUSIC!
LA LA LA LA LA LA LA!
LA LA LA LA LA LA LA LA!
SHALL WE TAKE A STROLL IN THE PARK BEFORE GOING HOME?
WITH PLEASURE!
IT WAS A BEAUTIFUL NIGHT WITH A GLOWING MOON.
LADY FELT HAPPY BEING WITH *TRAMP*. SHE FELT PROTECTED BY HIM.

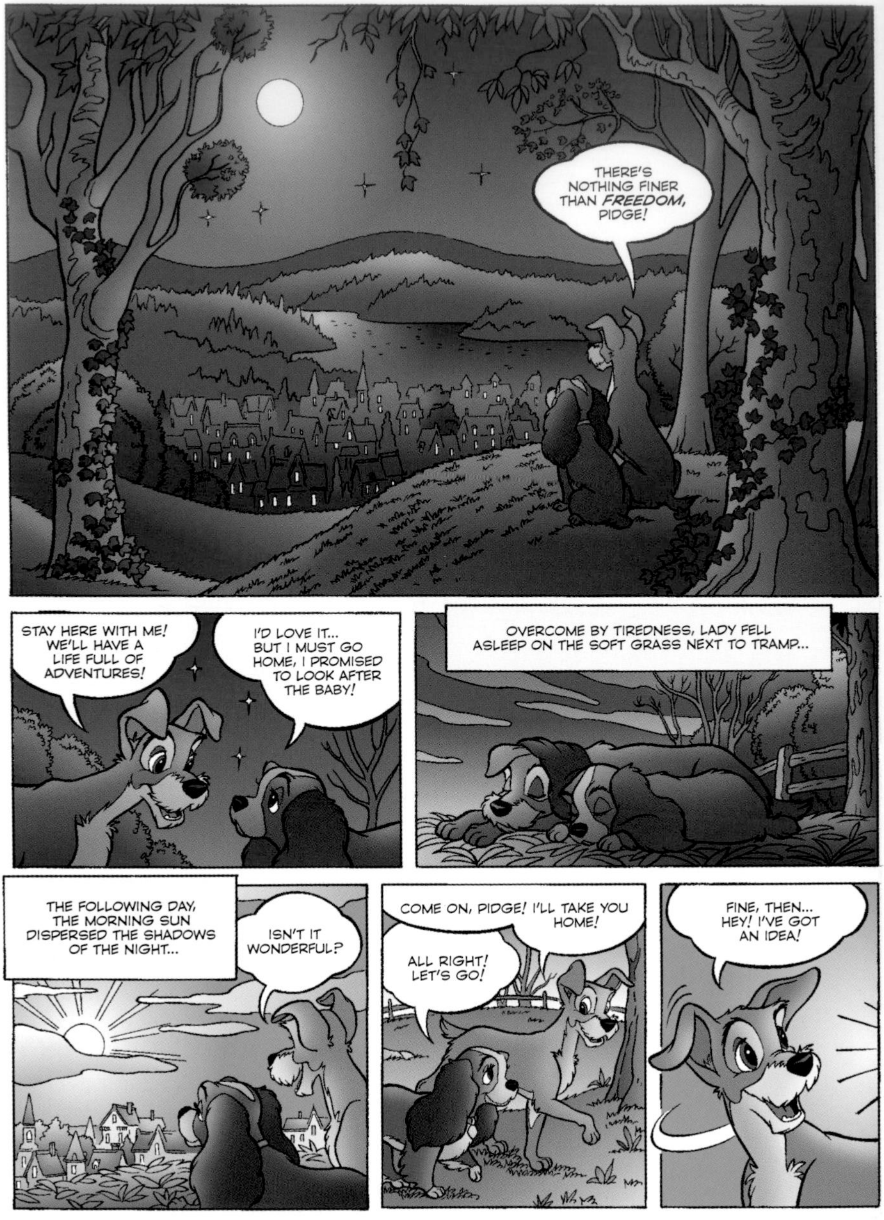
THERE'S NOTHING FINER THAN *FREEDOM*, PIDGE!
STAY HERE WITH ME! WE'LL HAVE A LIFE FULL OF ADVENTURES!
I'D LOVE IT... BUT I MUST GO HOME, I PROMISED TO LOOK AFTER THE BABY!
OVERCOME BY TIREDNESS, LADY FELL ASLEEP ON THE SOFT GRASS NEXT TO TRAMP...
THE FOLLOWING DAY, THE MORNING SUN DISPERSED THE SHADOWS OF THE NIGHT...
ISN'T IT WONDERFUL?
COME ON, PIDGE! I'LL TAKE YOU HOME!
ALL RIGHT! LET'S GO!
FINE, THEN... HEY! I'VE GOT AN IDEA!

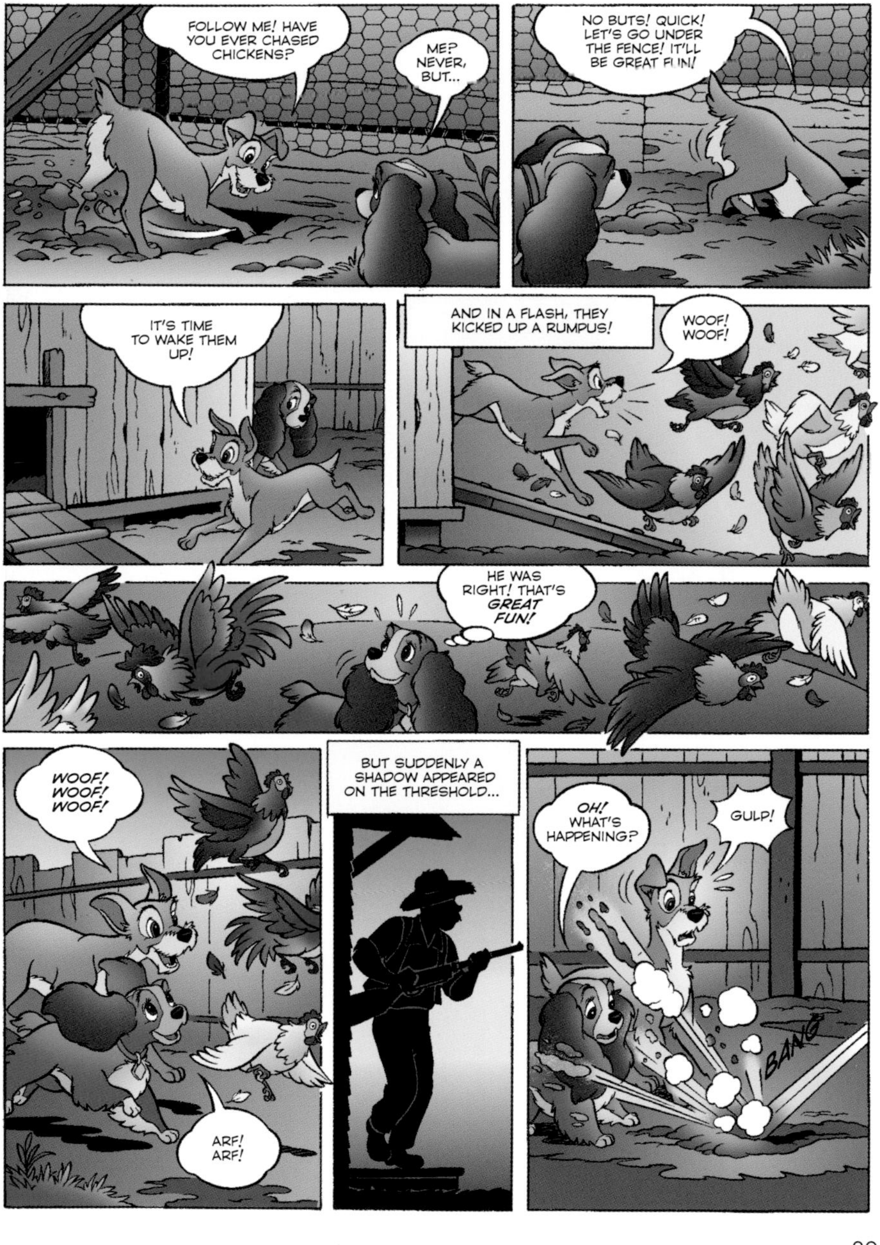
FOLLOW ME! HAVE YOU EVER CHASED CHICKENS?
ME? NEVER, BUT...
NO BUTS! QUICK! LET'S GO UNDER THE FENCE! IT'LL BE GREAT FUN!
IT'S TIME TO WAKE THEM UP!
AND IN A FLASH, THEY KICKED UP A RUMPUS!
WOOF! WOOF!
HE WAS RIGHT! THAT'S *GREAT FUN!*
WOOF! WOOF! WOOF!
ARF! ARF!
BUT SUDDENLY A SHADOW APPEARED ON THE THRESHOLD...
OH! WHAT'S HAPPENING?
GULP!
BANG

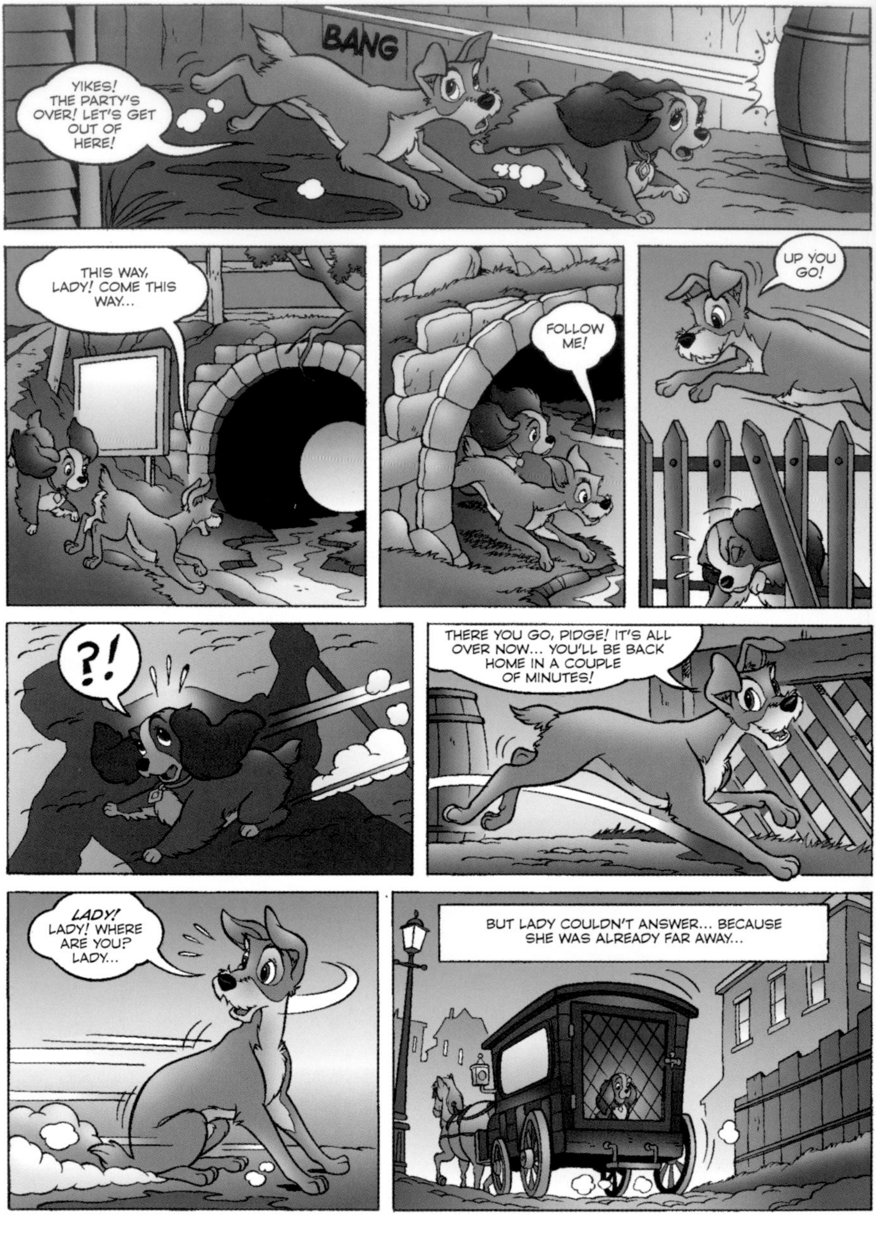
BANG
YIKES! THE PARTY'S OVER! LET'S GET OUT OF HERE!
THIS WAY, LADY! COME THIS WAY...
FOLLOW ME!
UP YOU GO!
?!
THERE YOU GO, PIDGE! IT'S ALL OVER NOW... YOU'LL BE BACK HOME IN A COUPLE OF MINUTES!
LADY! LADY! WHERE ARE YOU? LADY...
BUT LADY COULDN'T ANSWER... BECAUSE SHE WAS ALREADY FAR AWAY...

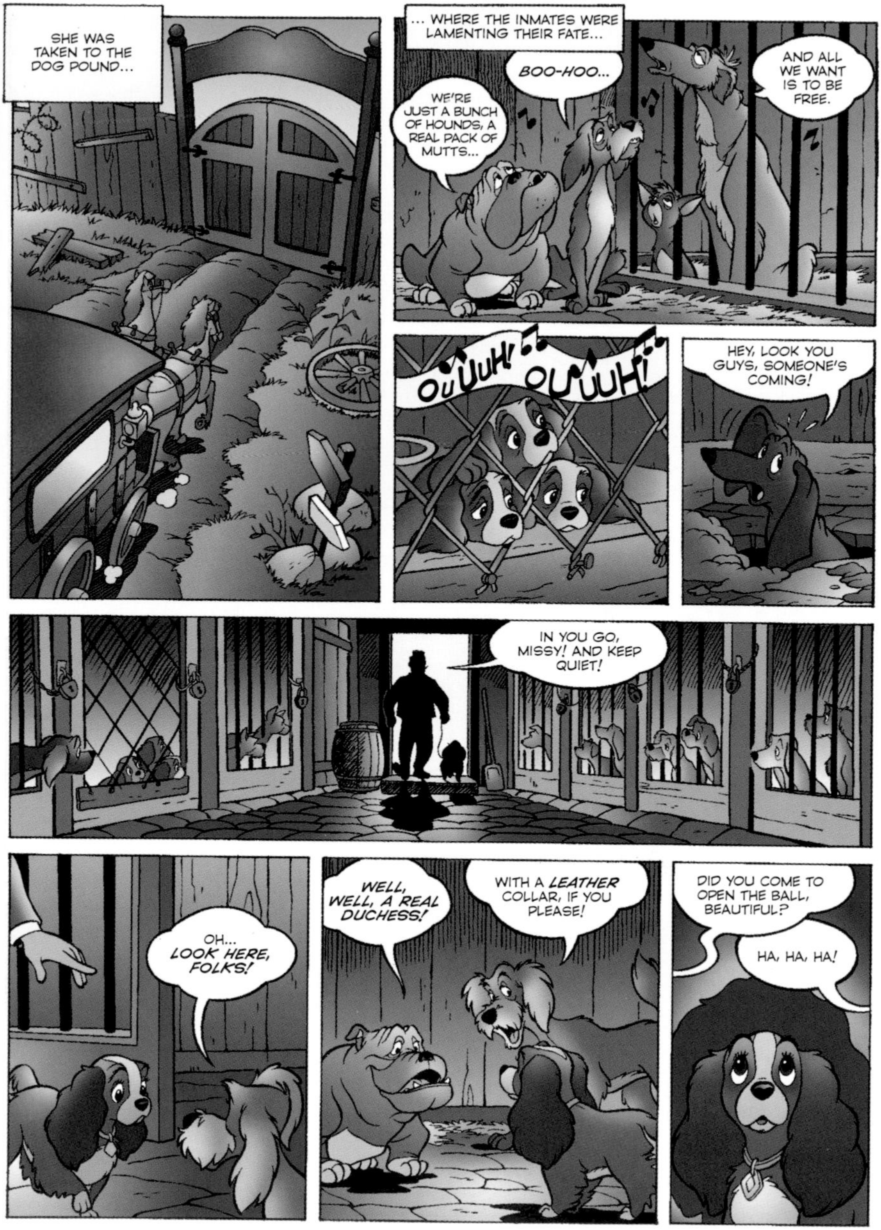
SHE WAS TAKEN TO THE DOG POUND...
... WHERE THE INMATES WERE LAMENTING THEIR FATE...
BOO-HOO...
WE'RE JUST A BUNCH OF HOUNDS, A REAL PACK OF MUTTS...
AND ALL WE WANT IS TO BE FREE.
OUUUH! OUUUH!
HEY, LOOK YOU GUYS, SOMEONE'S COMING!
IN YOU GO, MISSY! AND KEEP QUIET!
OH... LOOK HERE, FOLKS!
WELL, WELL, A REAL DUCHESS!
WITH A LEATHER COLLAR, IF YOU PLEASE!
DID YOU COME TO OPEN THE BALL, BEAUTIFUL?
HA, HA, HA!

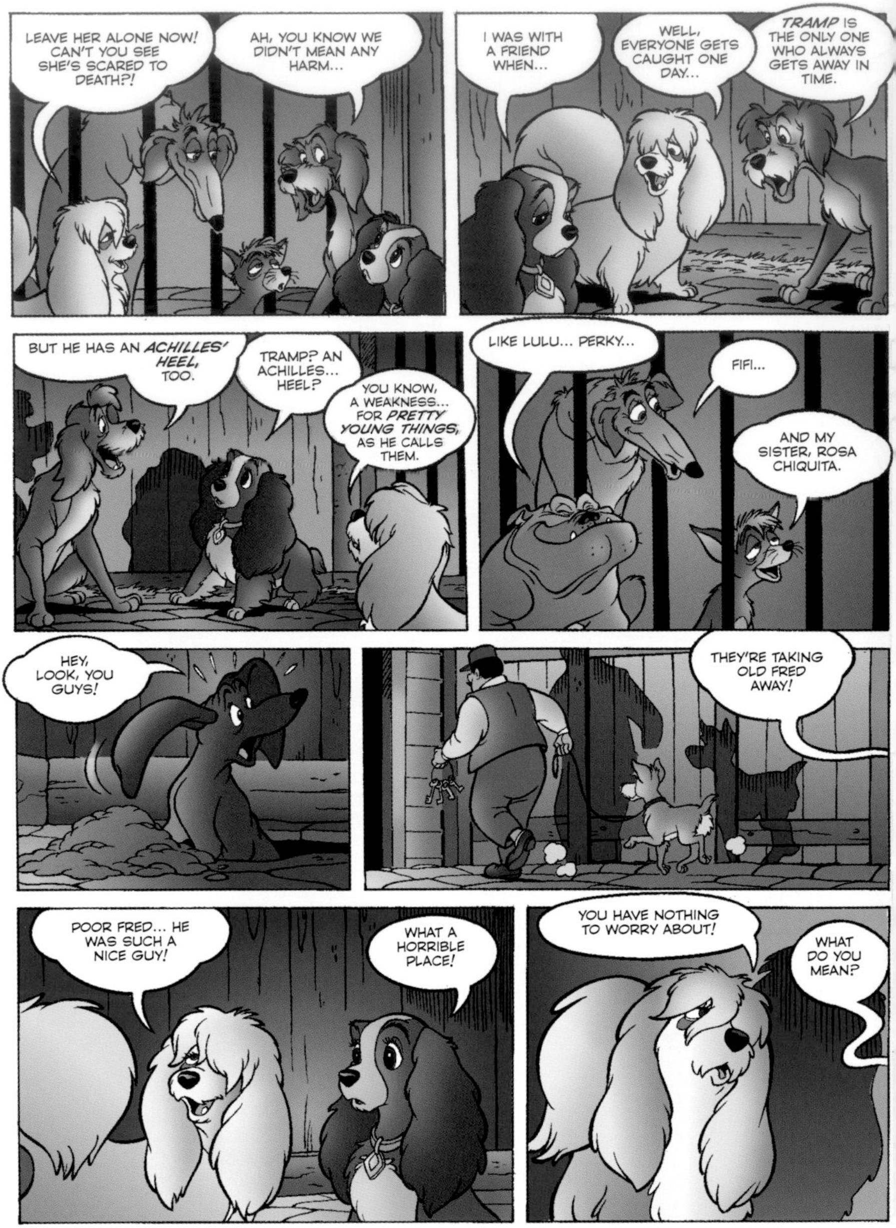
LEAVE HER ALONE NOW! CAN'T YOU SEE SHE'S SCARED TO DEATH?!
AH, YOU KNOW WE DIDN'T MEAN ANY HARM...
I WAS WITH A FRIEND WHEN...
WELL, EVERYONE GETS CAUGHT ONE DAY...
TRAMP IS THE ONLY ONE WHO ALWAYS GETS AWAY IN TIME.
BUT HE HAS AN ACHILLES' HEEL, TOO.
TRAMP? AN ACHILLES... HEEL?
YOU KNOW, A WEAKNESS... FOR PRETTY YOUNG THINGS, AS HE CALLS THEM.
LIKE LULU... PERKY...
FIFI...
AND MY SISTER, ROSA CHIQUITA.
HEY, LOOK, YOU GUYS!
THEY'RE TAKING OLD FRED AWAY!
POOR FRED... HE WAS SUCH A NICE GUY!
WHAT A HORRIBLE PLACE!
YOU HAVE NOTHING TO WORRY ABOUT!
WHAT DO YOU MEAN?

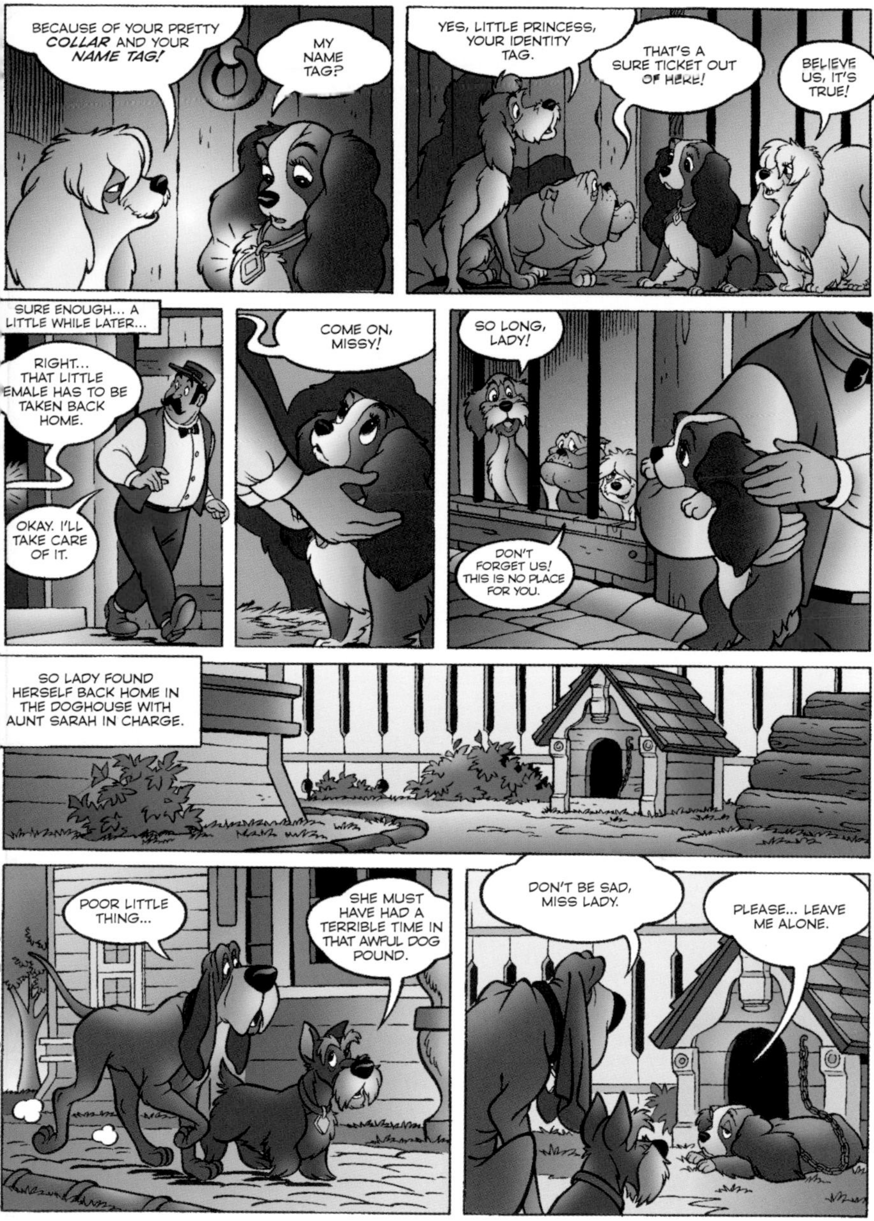

BECAUSE OF YOUR PRETTY COLLAR AND YOUR NAME TAG!
MY NAME TAG?
YES, LITTLE PRINCESS, YOUR IDENTITY TAG.
THAT'S A SURE TICKET OUT OF HERE!
BELIEVE US, IT'S TRUE!
SURE ENOUGH... A LITTLE WHILE LATER...
RIGHT... THAT LITTLE EMALE HAS TO BE TAKEN BACK HOME.
OKAY. I'LL TAKE CARE OF IT.
COME ON, MISSY!
SO LONG, LADY!
DON'T FORGET US! THIS IS NO PLACE FOR YOU.
SO LADY FOUND HERSELF BACK HOME IN THE DOGHOUSE WITH AUNT SARAH IN CHARGE.
POOR LITTLE THING...
SHE MUST HAVE HAD A TERRIBLE TIME IN THAT AWFUL DOG POUND.
DON'T BE SAD, MISS LADY.
PLEASE... LEAVE ME ALONE.

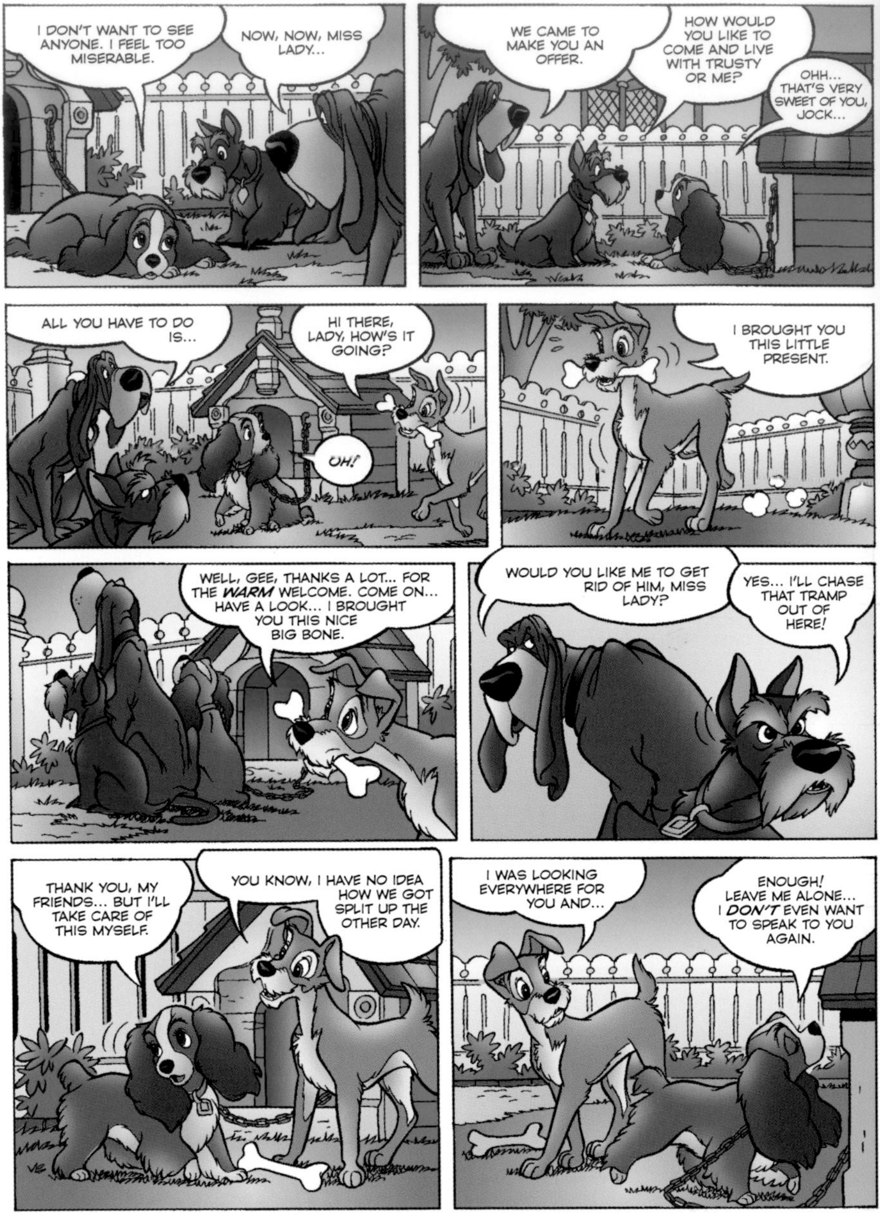

I DON'T WANT TO SEE ANYONE. I FEEL TOO MISERABLE.
NOW, NOW, MISS LADY...
WE CAME TO MAKE YOU AN OFFER.
HOW WOULD YOU LIKE TO COME AND LIVE WITH TRUSTY OR ME?
OHH... THAT'S VERY SWEET OF YOU, JOCK...
ALL YOU HAVE TO DO IS...
HI THERE, LADY, HOW'S IT GOING?
OH!
I BROUGHT YOU THIS LITTLE PRESENT.
WELL, GEE, THANKS A LOT... FOR THE *WARM* WELCOME. COME ON... HAVE A LOOK... I BROUGHT YOU THIS NICE BIG BONE.
WOULD YOU LIKE ME TO GET RID OF HIM, MISS LADY?
YES... I'LL CHASE THAT TRAMP OUT OF HERE!
THANK YOU, MY FRIENDS... BUT I'LL TAKE CARE OF THIS MYSELF.
YOU KNOW, I HAVE NO IDEA HOW WE GOT SPLIT UP THE OTHER DAY.
I WAS LOOKING EVERYWHERE FOR YOU AND...
ENOUGH! LEAVE ME ALONE... I *DON'T* EVEN WANT TO SPEAK TO YOU AGAIN.

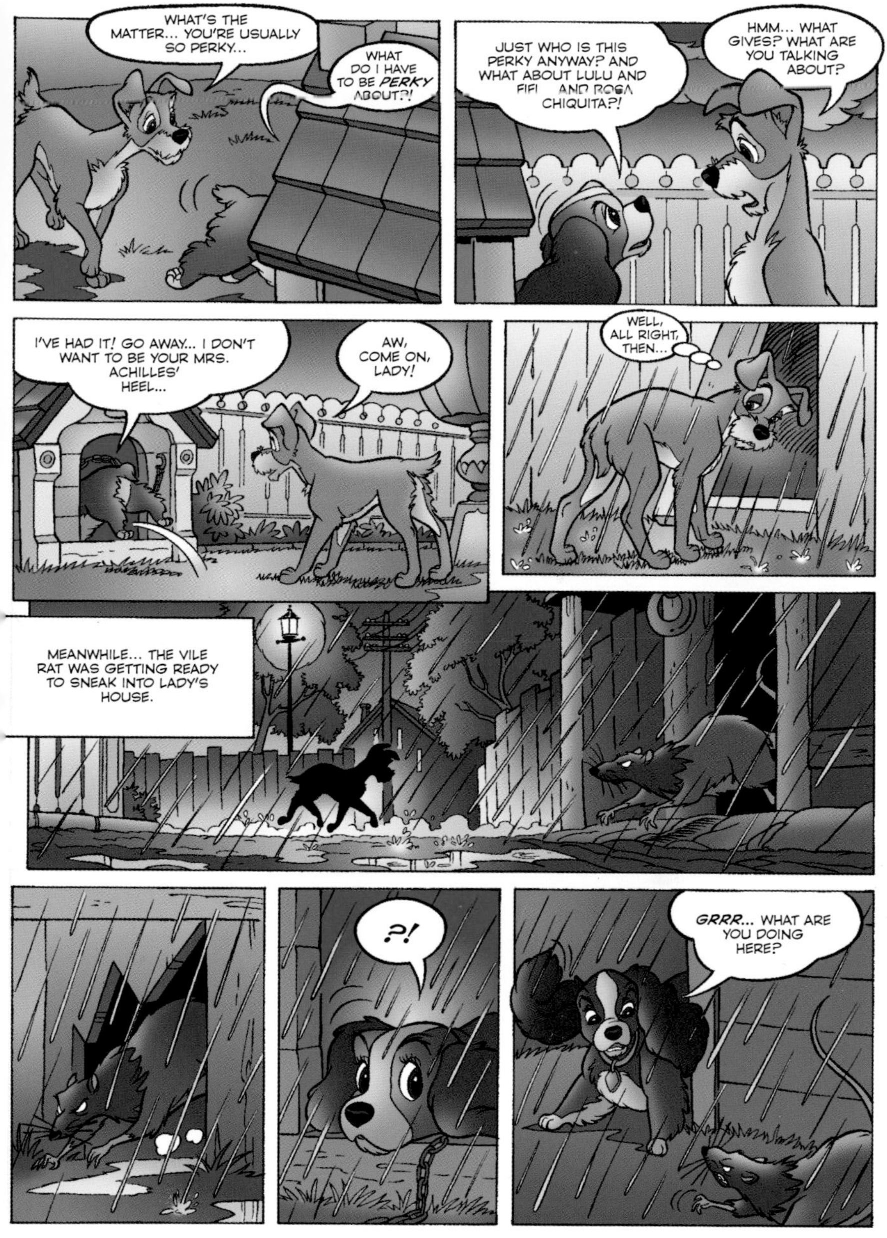
WHAT'S THE MATTER... YOU'RE USUALLY SO PERKY...
WHAT DO I HAVE TO BE PERKY ABOUT?!
JUST WHO IS THIS PERKY ANYWAY? AND WHAT ABOUT LULU AND FIFI... AND ROSA CHIQUITA?!
HMM... WHAT GIVES? WHAT ARE YOU TALKING ABOUT?
I'VE HAD IT! GO AWAY... I DON'T WANT TO BE YOUR MRS. ACHILLES' HEEL...
AW, COME ON, LADY!
WELL, ALL RIGHT, THEN...
MEANWHILE... THE VILE RAT WAS GETTING READY TO SNEAK INTO LADY'S HOUSE.
?!
GRRR... WHAT ARE YOU DOING HERE?

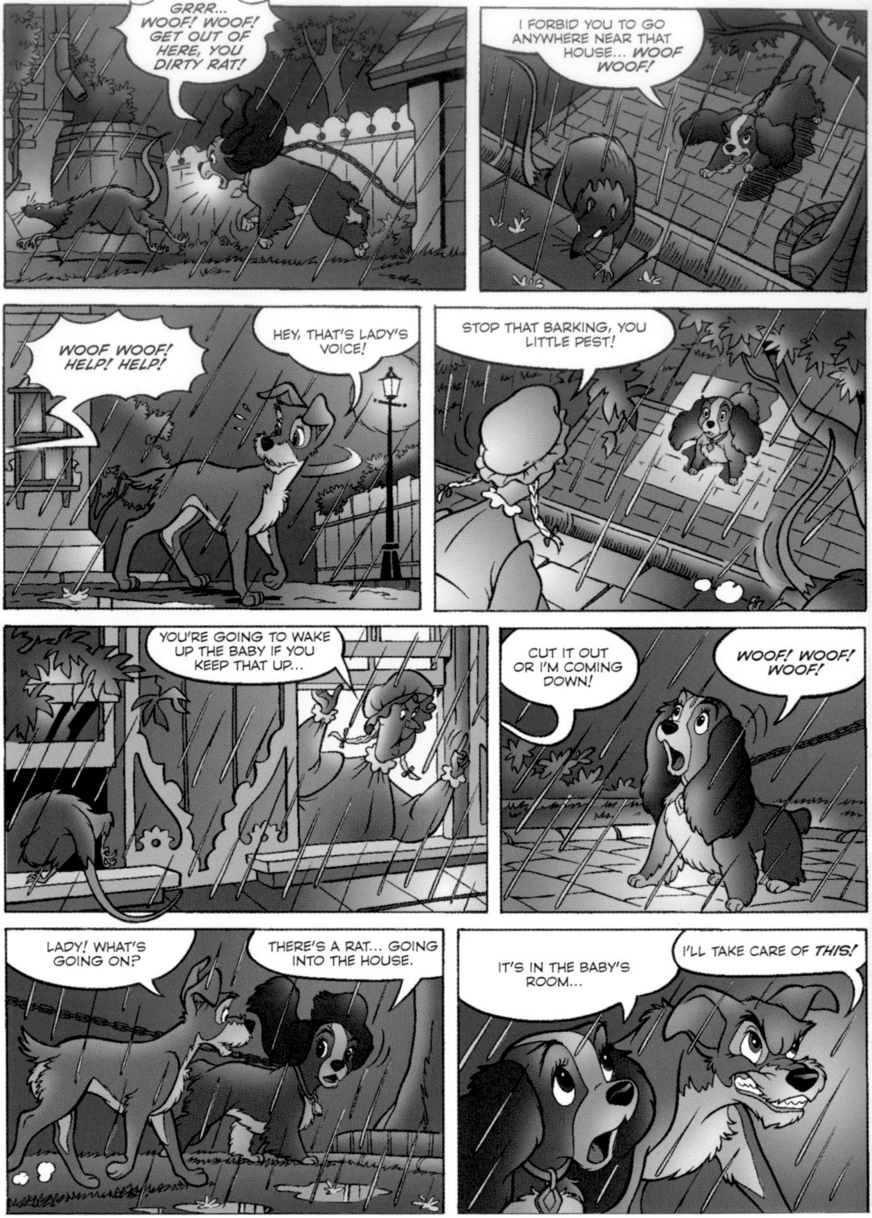
GRRR... WOOF! WOOF! GET OUT OF HERE, YOU DIRTY RAT!
I FORBID YOU TO GO ANYWHERE NEAR THAT HOUSE... WOOF WOOF!
WOOF WOOF! HELP! HELP!
HEY, THAT'S LADY'S VOICE!
STOP THAT BARKING, YOU LITTLE PEST!
YOU'RE GOING TO WAKE UP THE BABY IF YOU KEEP THAT UP...
CUT IT OUT OR I'M COMING DOWN!
WOOF! WOOF! WOOF!
LADY! WHAT'S GOING ON?
THERE'S A RAT... GOING INTO THE HOUSE.
IT'S IN THE BABY'S ROOM...
I'LL TAKE CARE OF THIS!

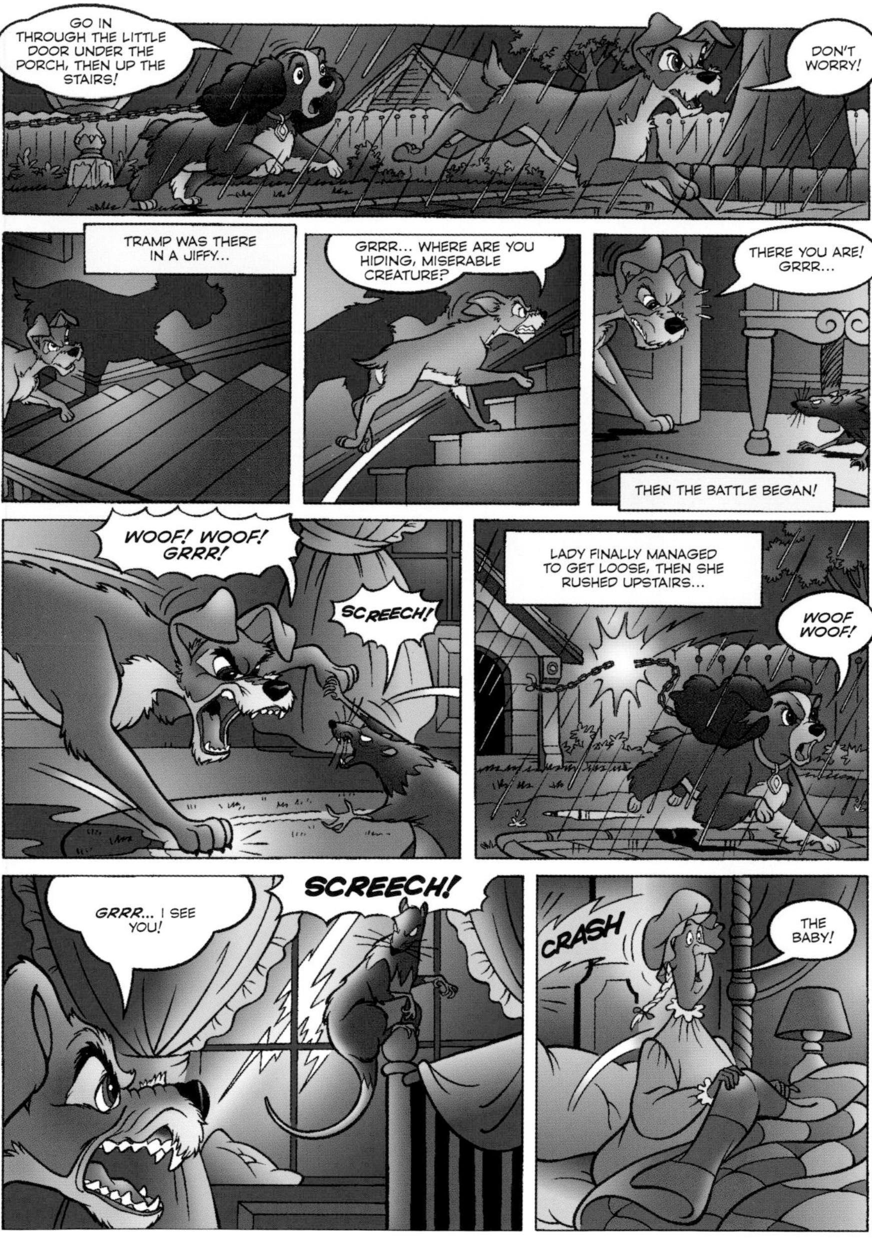
GO IN THROUGH THE LITTLE DOOR UNDER THE PORCH, THEN UP THE STAIRS!
DON'T WORRY!
TRAMP WAS THERE IN A JIFFY...
GRRR... WHERE ARE YOU HIDING, MISERABLE CREATURE?
THERE YOU ARE! GRRR...
THEN THE BATTLE BEGAN!
WOOF! WOOF! GRRR!
SCREECH!
LADY FINALLY MANAGED TO GET LOOSE, THEN SHE RUSHED UPSTAIRS...
WOOF WOOF!
GRRR... I SEE YOU!
SCREECH!
CRASH
THE BABY!

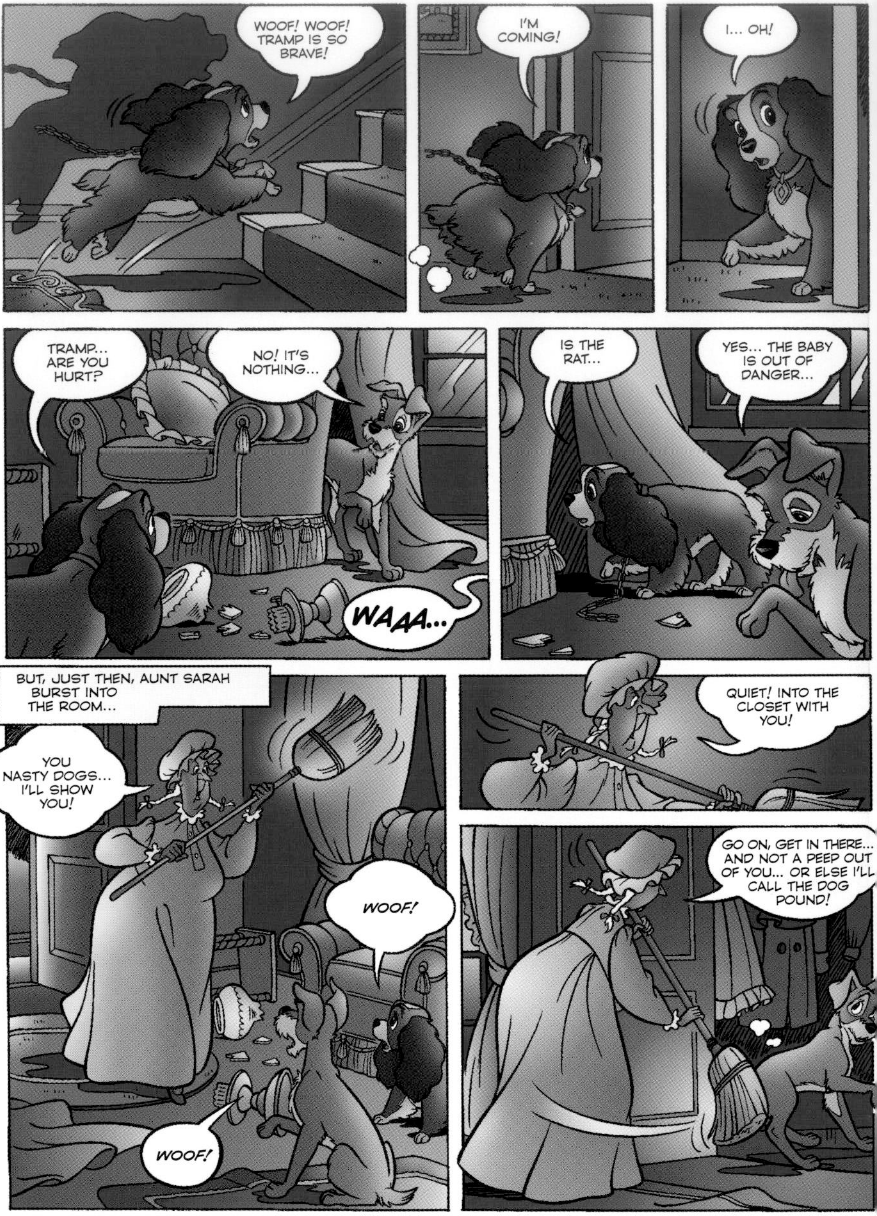
WOOF! WOOF! TRAMP IS SO BRAVE!
I'M COMING!
I... OH!
TRAMP... ARE YOU HURT?
NO! IT'S NOTHING...
WAAA...
IS THE RAT...
YES... THE BABY IS OUT OF DANGER...
BUT, JUST THEN, AUNT SARAH BURST INTO THE ROOM...
YOU NASTY DOGS... I'LL SHOW YOU!
WOOF!
WOOF!
QUIET! INTO THE CLOSET WITH YOU!
GO ON, GET IN THERE... AND NOT A PEEP OUT OF YOU... OR ELSE I'LL CALL THE DOG POUND!

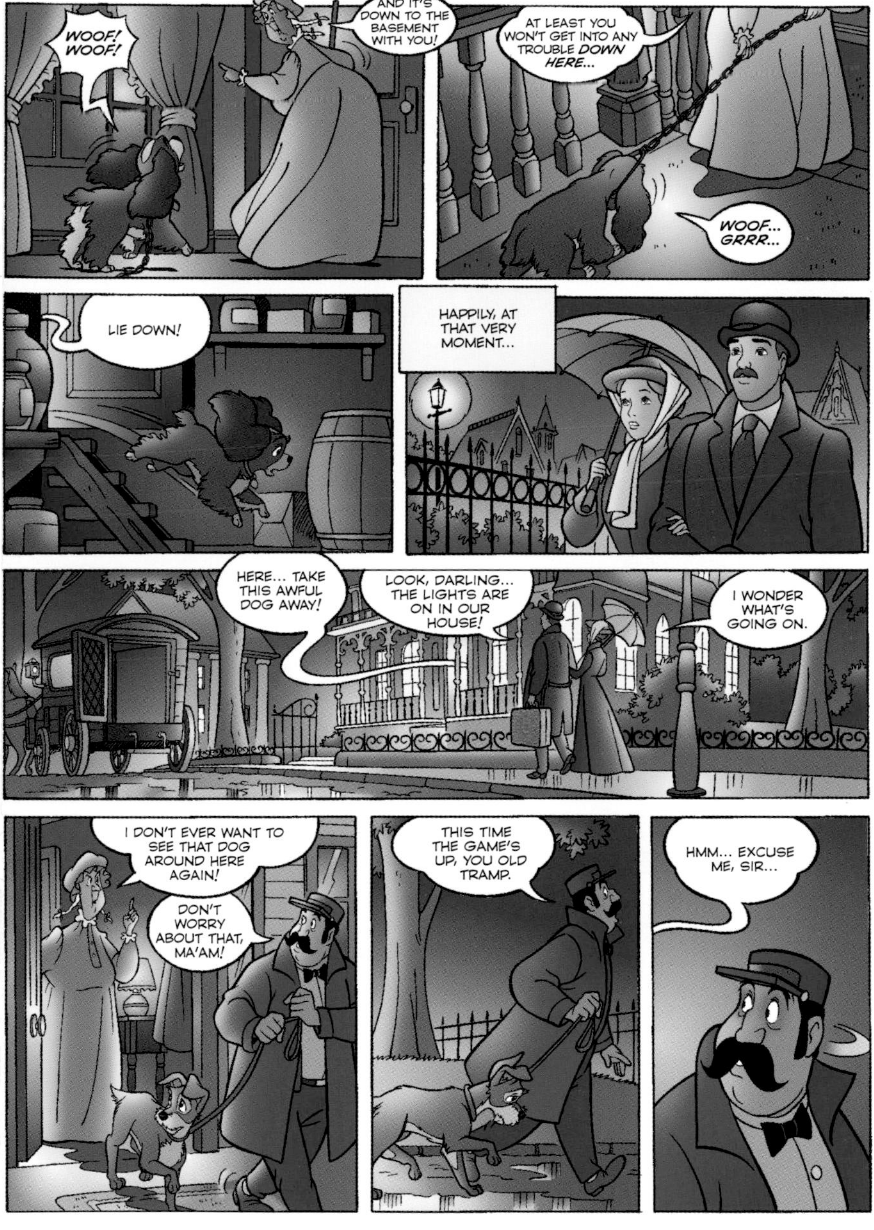
WOOF! WOOF!
AND IT'S DOWN TO THE BASEMENT WITH YOU!
AT LEAST YOU WON'T GET INTO ANY TROUBLE *DOWN HERE*...
WOOF... GRRR...
LIE DOWN!
HAPPILY, AT THAT VERY MOMENT...
HERE... TAKE THIS AWFUL DOG AWAY!
LOOK, DARLING... THE LIGHTS ARE ON IN OUR HOUSE!
I WONDER WHAT'S GOING ON.
I DON'T EVER WANT TO SEE THAT DOG AROUND HERE AGAIN!
DON'T WORRY ABOUT THAT, MA'AM!
THIS TIME THE GAME'S UP, YOU OLD TRAMP.
HMM... EXCUSE ME, SIR...

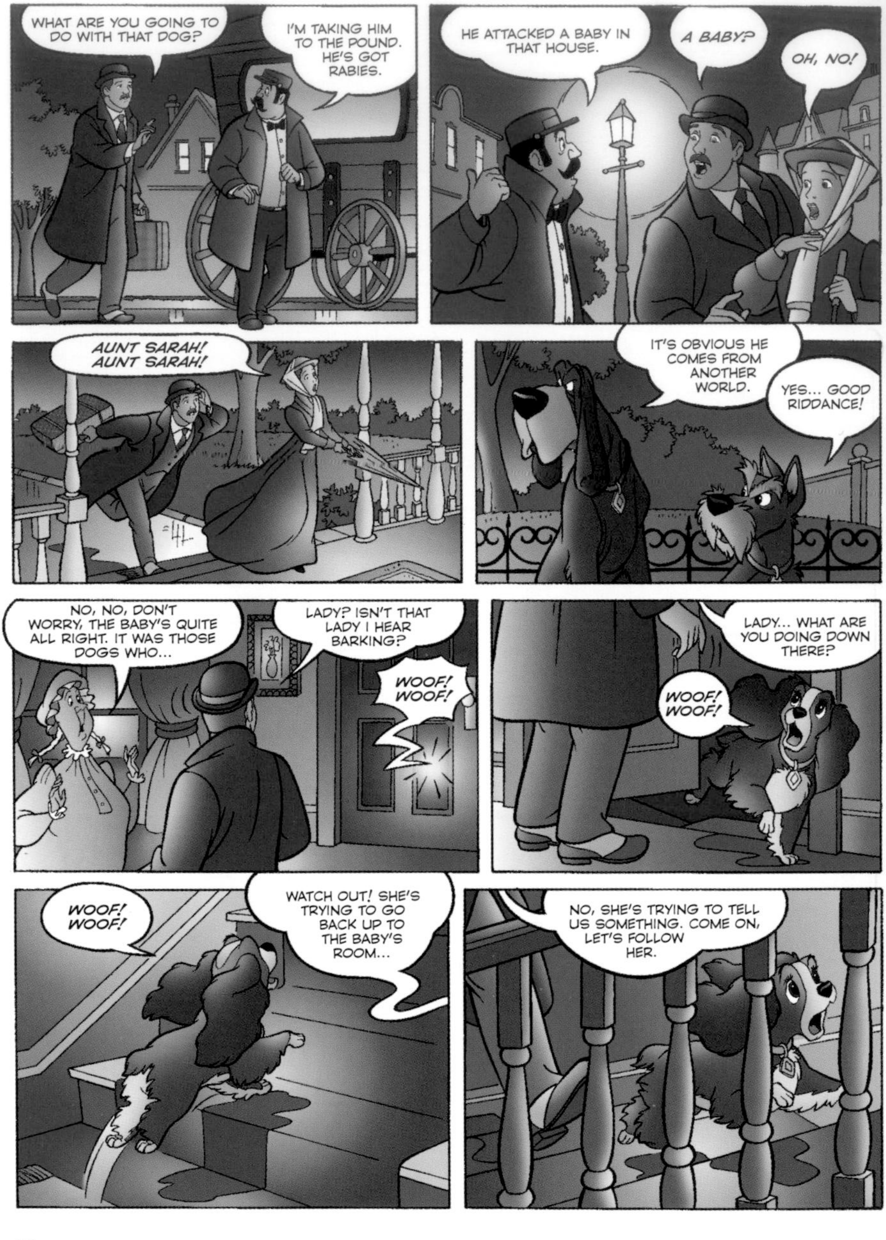
WHAT ARE YOU GOING TO DO WITH THAT DOG?
I'M TAKING HIM TO THE POUND. HE'S GOT RABIES.
HE ATTACKED A BABY IN THAT HOUSE.
A BABY?
OH, NO!
AUNT SARAH! AUNT SARAH!
IT'S OBVIOUS HE COMES FROM ANOTHER WORLD.
YES... GOOD RIDDANCE!
NO, NO, DON'T WORRY, THE BABY'S QUITE ALL RIGHT. IT WAS THOSE DOGS WHO...
LADY? ISN'T THAT LADY I HEAR BARKING?
WOOF! WOOF!
LADY... WHAT ARE YOU DOING DOWN THERE?
WOOF! WOOF!
WOOF! WOOF!
WATCH OUT! SHE'S TRYING TO GO BACK UP TO THE BABY'S ROOM...
NO, SHE'S TRYING TO TELL US SOMETHING. COME ON, LET'S FOLLOW HER.

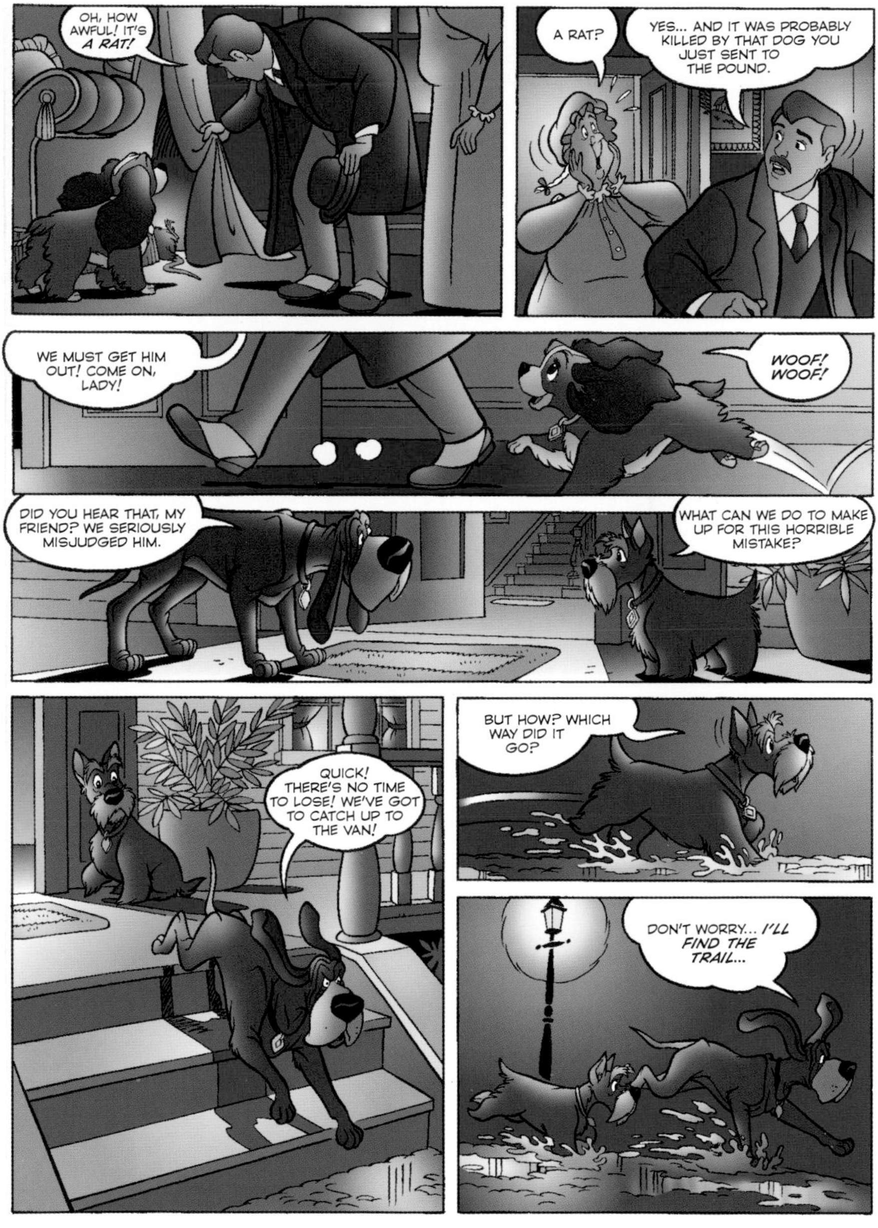
OH, HOW AWFUL! IT'S A RAT!
A RAT?
YES... AND IT WAS PROBABLY KILLED BY THAT DOG YOU JUST SENT TO THE POUND.
WE MUST GET HIM OUT! COME ON, LADY!
WOOF! WOOF!
DID YOU HEAR THAT, MY FRIEND? WE SERIOUSLY MISJUDGED HIM.
WHAT CAN WE DO TO MAKE UP FOR THIS HORRIBLE MISTAKE?
QUICK! THERE'S NO TIME TO LOSE! WE'VE GOT TO CATCH UP TO THE VAN!
BUT HOW? WHICH WAY DID IT GO?
DON'T WORRY... I'LL FIND THE TRAIL...

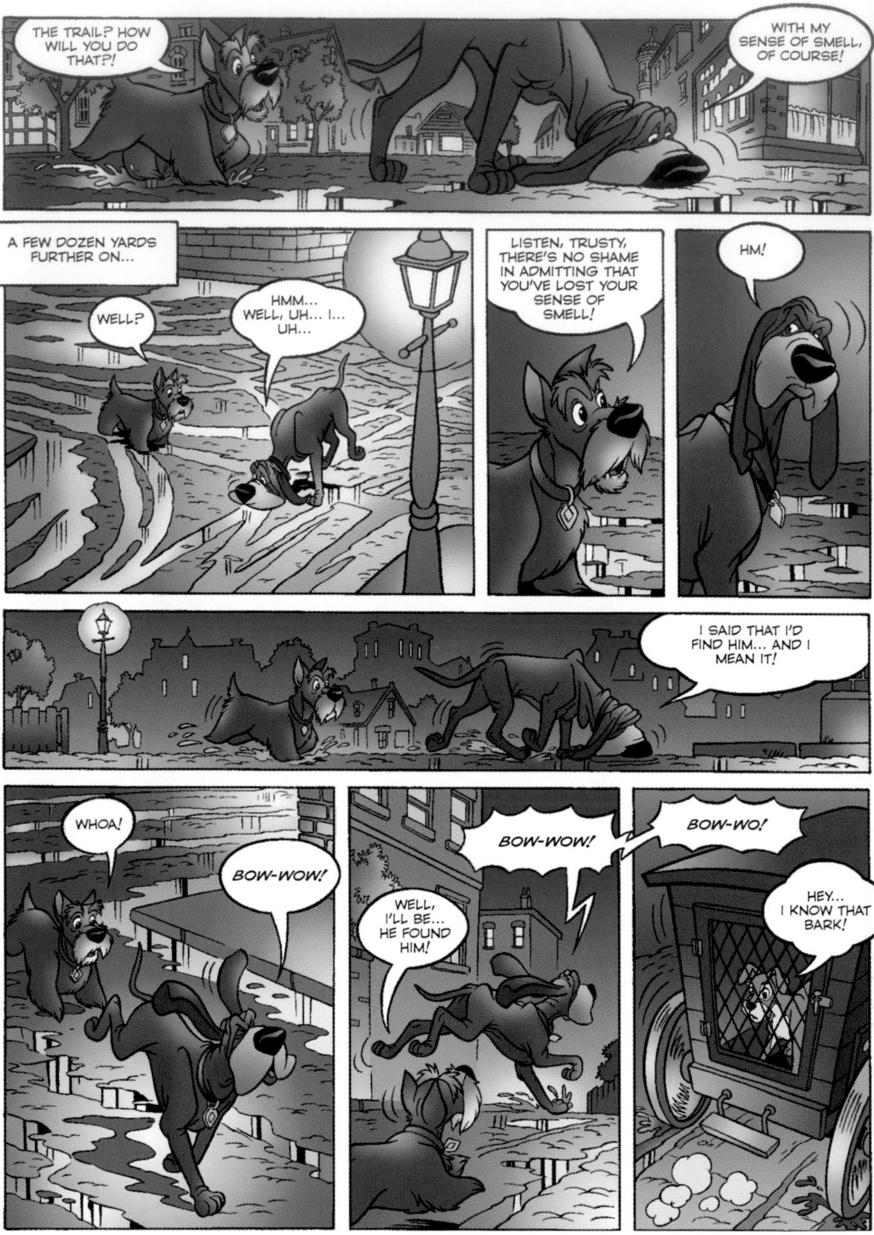
THE TRAIL? HOW WILL YOU DO THAT?!
WITH MY SENSE OF SMELL, OF COURSE!
A FEW DOZEN YARDS FURTHER ON...
WELL?
HMM... WELL, UH... I... UH...
LISTEN, TRUSTY, THERE'S NO SHAME IN ADMITTING THAT YOU'VE LOST YOUR SENSE OF SMELL!
HM!
I SAID THAT I'D FIND HIM... AND I MEAN IT!
WHOA!
BOW-WOW!
BOW-WOW!
WELL, I'LL BE... HE FOUND HIM!
BOW-WO!
HEY... I KNOW THAT BARK!

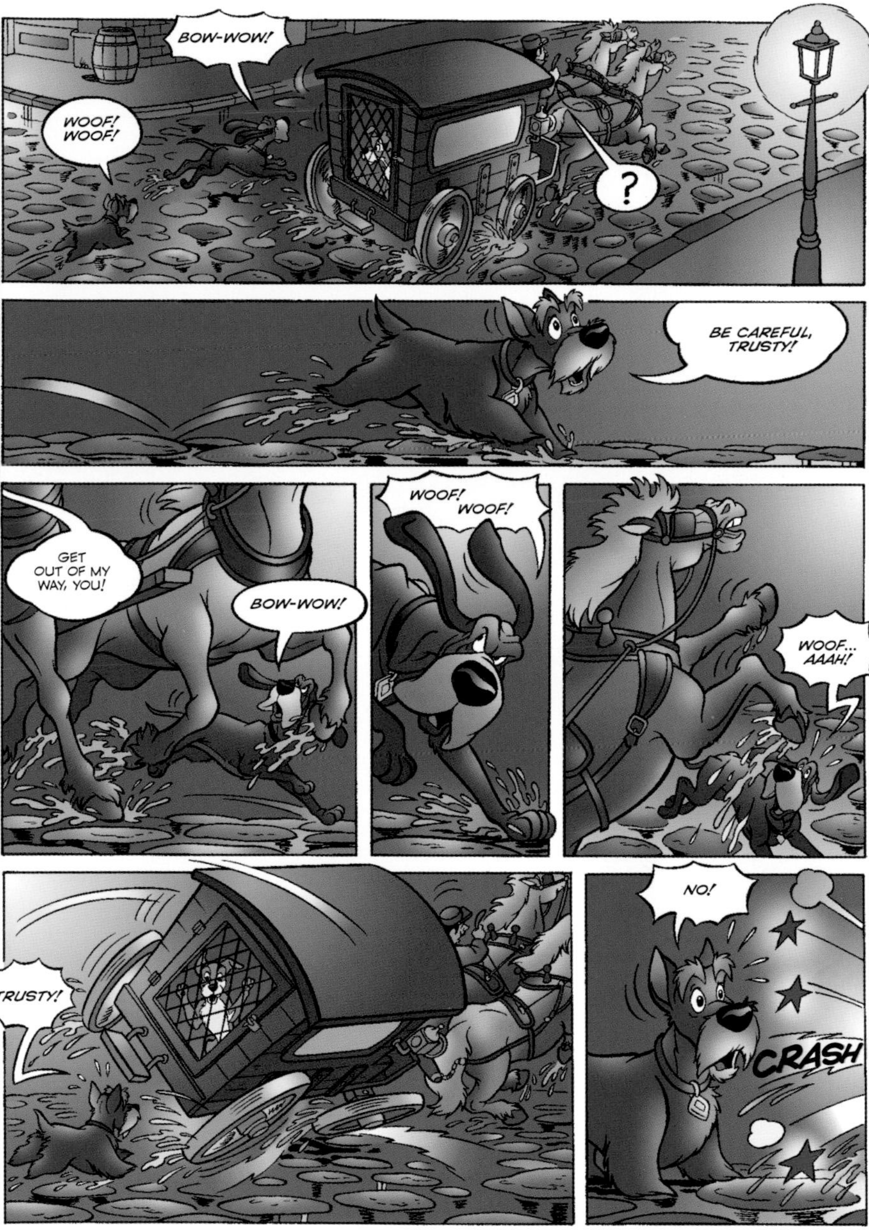
BOW-WOW!
WOOF! WOOF!
?
BE CAREFUL, TRUSTY!
GET OUT OF MY WAY, YOU!
BOW-WOW!
WOOF! WOOF!
WOOF... AAAH!
TRUSTY!
NO!
CRASH

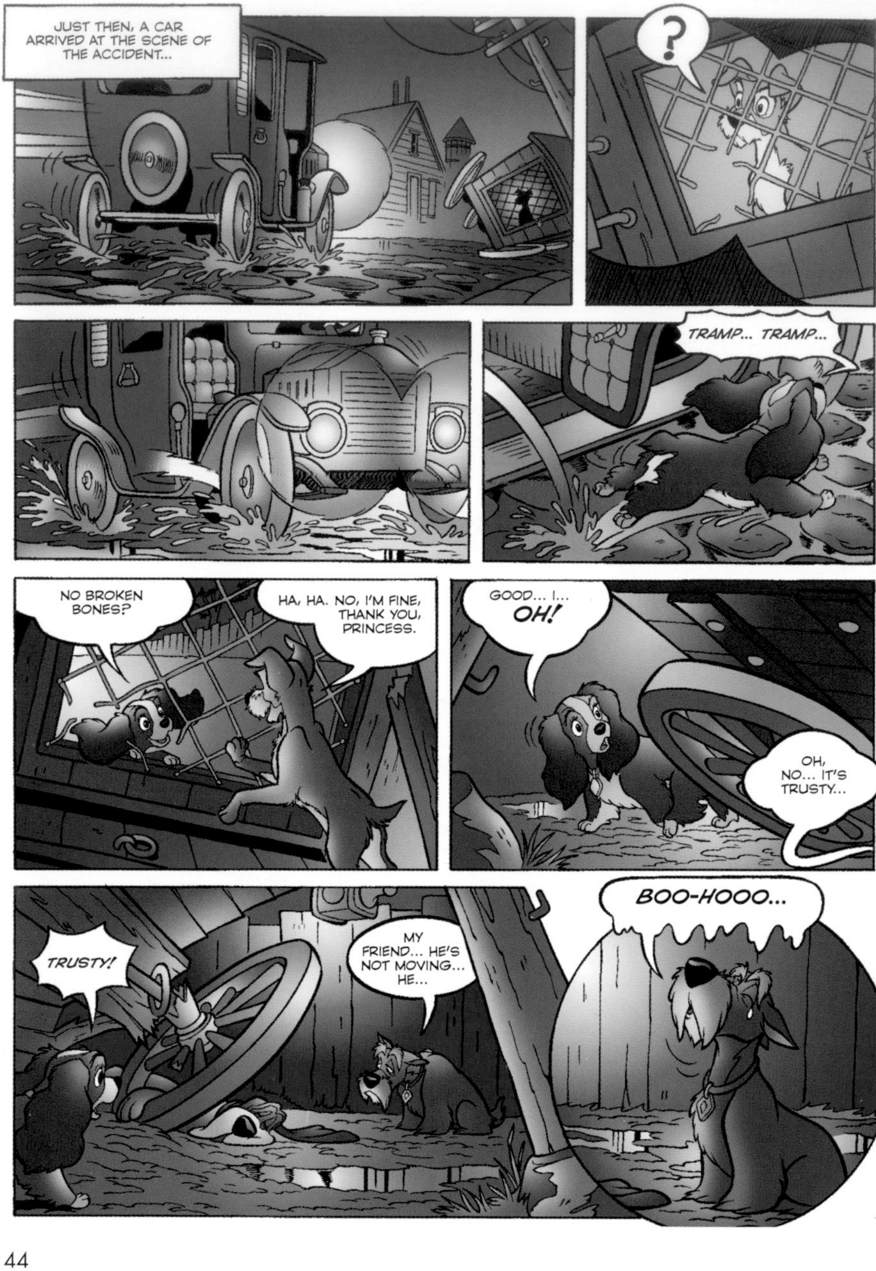

JUST THEN, A CAR ARRIVED AT THE SCENE OF THE ACCIDENT...
?
TRAMP... TRAMP...
NO BROKEN BONES?
HA, HA. NO, I'M FINE, THANK YOU, PRINCESS.
GOOD... I... OH!
OH, NO... IT'S TRUSTY...
TRUSTY!
MY FRIEND... HE'S NOT MOVING... HE...
BOO-HOOO...

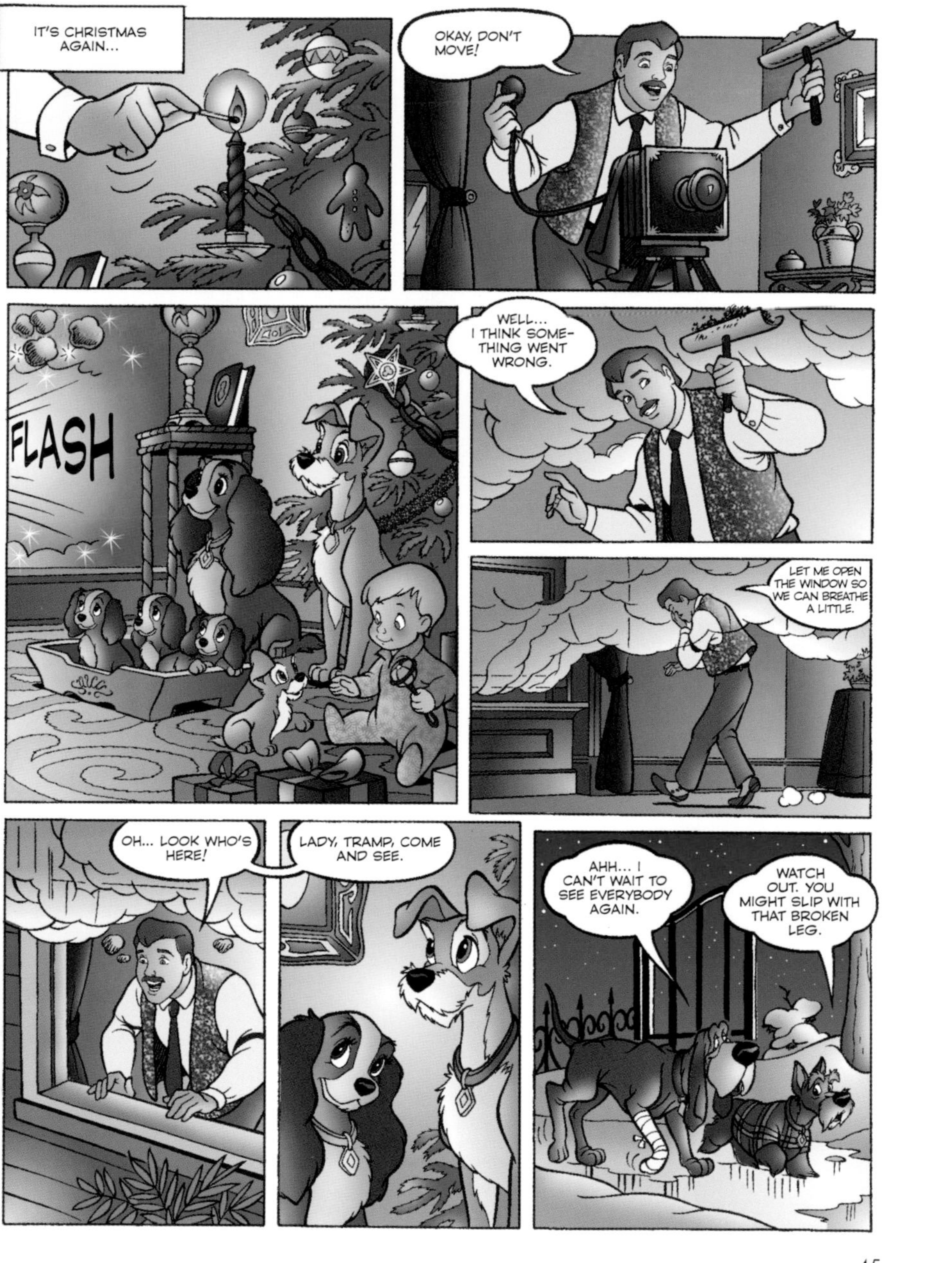
IT'S CHRISTMAS AGAIN...
OKAY, DON'T MOVE!
FLASH
WELL... I THINK SOME-THING WENT WRONG.
LET ME OPEN THE WINDOW SO WE CAN BREATHE A LITTLE.
OH... LOOK WHO'S HERE!
LADY, TRAMP, COME AND SEE.
AHH... I CAN'T WAIT TO SEE EVERYBODY AGAIN.
WATCH OUT. YOU MIGHT SLIP WITH THAT BROKEN LEG.

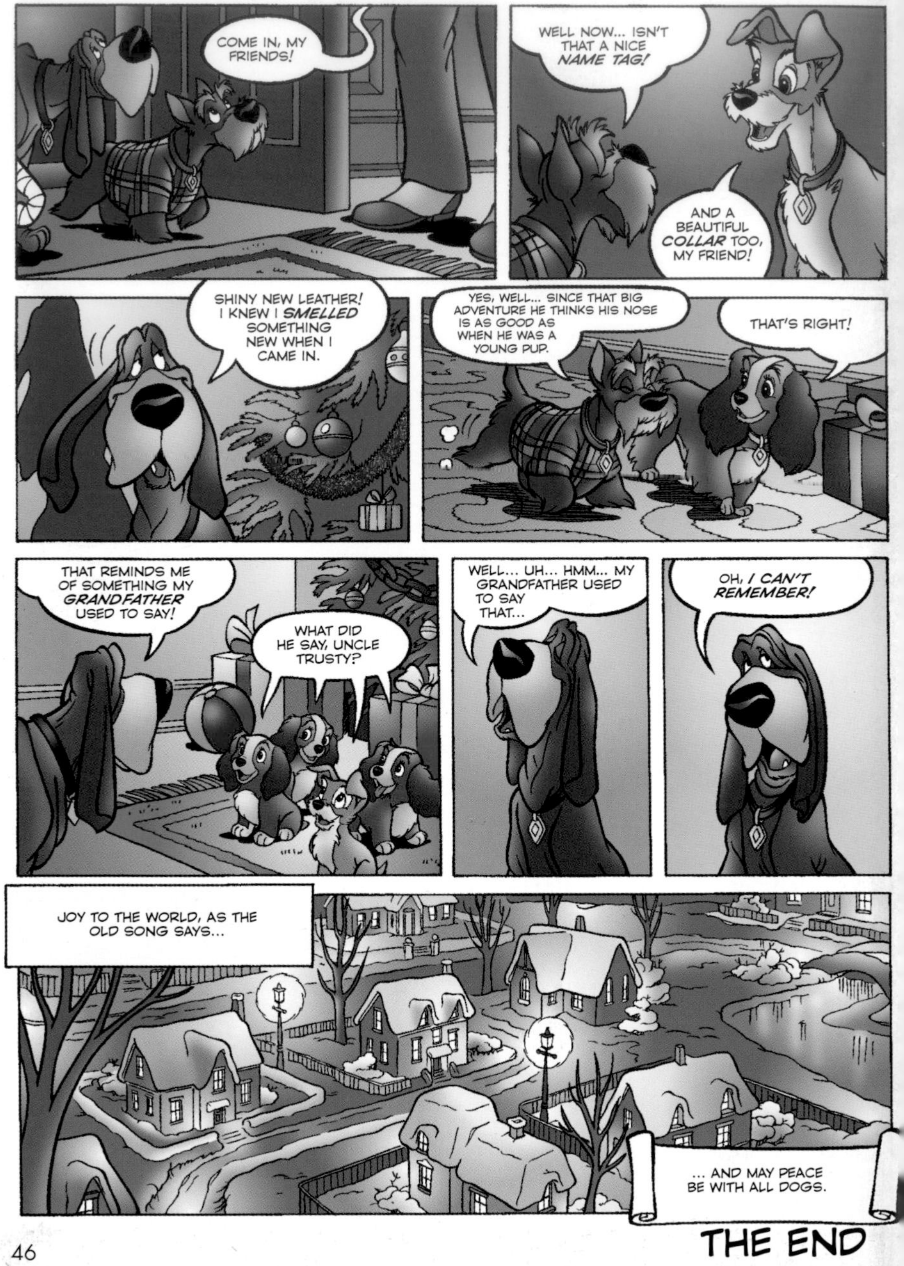

COME IN, MY FRIENDS!
WELL NOW... ISN'T THAT A NICE NAME TAG!
AND A BEAUTIFUL COLLAR TOO, MY FRIEND!
SHINY NEW LEATHER! I KNEW I SMELLED SOMETHING NEW WHEN I CAME IN.
YES, WELL... SINCE THAT BIG ADVENTURE HE THINKS HIS NOSE IS AS GOOD AS WHEN HE WAS A YOUNG PUP.
THAT'S RIGHT!
THAT REMINDS ME OF SOMETHING MY GRANDFATHER USED TO SAY!
WHAT DID HE SAY, UNCLE TRUSTY?
WELL... UH... HMM... MY GRANDFATHER USED TO SAY THAT...
OH, I CAN'T REMEMBER!
JOY TO THE WORLD, AS THE OLD SONG SAYS...
... AND MAY PEACE BE WITH ALL DOGS.

THE END

WRITER
François Corteggiani

ART
Mario Cortes

DARK HORSE BOOKS
PRESIDENT AND PUBLISHER **Mike Richardson**
COLLECTION EDITOR **Freddye Miller**   COLLECTION ASSISTANT EDITOR **Judy Khuu**
DESIGNER **Jen Edwards**   DIGITAL ART TECHNICIAN **Samantha Hummer**

Neil Hankerson Executive Vice President • Tom Weddle Chief Financial Officer • Randy Stradley Vice President of Publishing • Nick McWhorter Chief Business Development Officer • Dale LaFountain Chief Information Officer • Matt Parkinson Vice President of Marketing • Cara Niece Vice President of Production and Scheduling • Mark Bernardi Vice President of Book Trade and Digital Sales • Ken Lizzi General Counsel • Dave Marshall Editor in Chief • Davey Estrada Editorial Director • Chris Warner Senior Books Editor • Cary Grazzini Director of Specialty Projects • Lia Ribacchi Art Director • Vanessa Todd-Holmes Director of Print Purchasing • Matt Dryer Director of Digital Art and Prepress • Michael Gombos Senior Director of Licensed Publications • Kari Yadro Director of Custom Programs • Kari Torson Director of International Licensing • Sean Brice Director of Trade Sales

DISNEY PUBLISHING WORLDWIDE GLOBAL MAGAZINES, COMICS AND PARTWORKS

PUBLISHER Lynn Waggoner • EDITORIAL TEAM Bianca Coletti (Director, Magazines), Guido Frazzini (Director, Comics), Carlotta Quattrocolo (Executive Editor), Stefano Ambrosio (Executive Editor, New IP), Camilla Vedove (Senior Manager, Editorial Development), Behnoosh Khalili (Senior Editor), Julie Dorris (Senior Editor), Mina Riazi (Assistant Editor), Gabriela Capasso (Assistant Editor) • DESIGN Enrico Soave (Senior Designer) • ART Ken Shue (VP, Global Art), Manny Mederos (Senior Illustration Manager, Comics and Magazines), Roberto Santillo (Creative Director), Marco Ghiglione (Creative Manager), Stefano Attardi (Illustration Manager) • PORTFOLIO MANAGEMENT Olivia Ciancarelli (Director) • BUSINESS & MARKETING Mariantonietta Galla (Senior Manager, Franchise), Virpi Korhonen (Editorial Manager)

Published by Dark Horse Books
A division of Dark Horse Comics LLC
10956 SE Main Street | Milwaukie, OR 97222

DarkHorse.com

To find a comics shop in your area, visit comicshoplocator.com

First Dark Horse Books edition: April 2020
ISBN 978-1-50671-734-0 | Digital ISBN 978-1-50671-743-2

1 3 5 7 9 10 8 6 4 2
Printed in China

LOOKING FOR BOOKS FOR YOUNGER READERS?

$7.99 each!

EACH VOLUME INCLUDES A SECTION OF FUN ACTIVITIES!

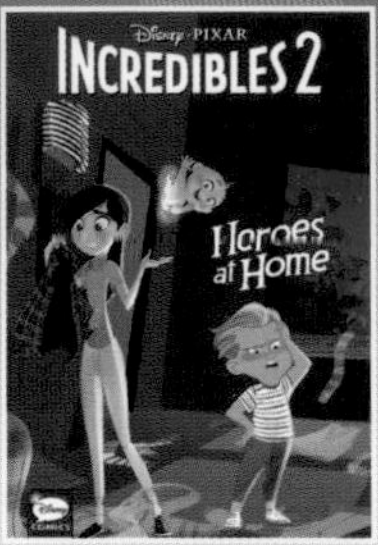

Disney·PIXAR
INCREDIBLES 2
Heroes at Home

DISNEY•PIXAR INCREDIBLES 2: HEROES AT HOME
ISBN 978-1-50670-943-7
Being part of a Super family means helping out at home, too. Can Violet and Dash pick up groceries and secretly stop some bad guys? And can they clean up the house while Jack-Jack is "sleeping"?

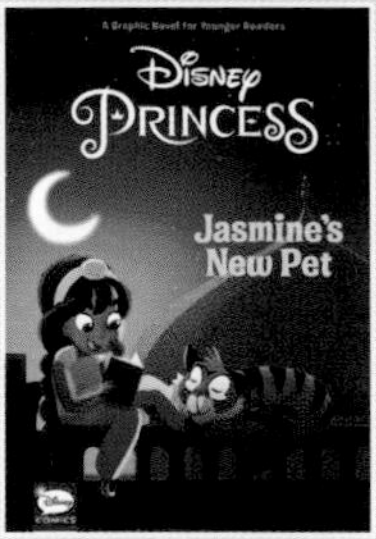

A Graphic Novel for Younger Readers
Disney
PRINCESS
Jasmine's New Pet

DISNEY PRINCESS: JASMINE'S NEW PET
ISBN 978-1-50671-052-5
Jasmine has a new pet tiger, Rajah, but he's not quite ready for palace life. Will she be able to train the young cub before the Sultan finds him another home?

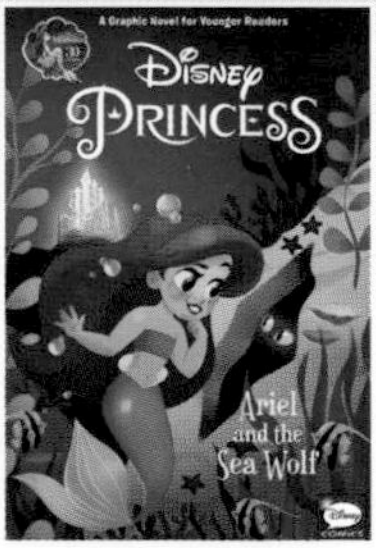

A Graphic Novel for Younger Readers
Disney
PRINCESS
Ariel and the Sea Wolf

DISNEY PRINCESS: ARIEL AND THE SEA WOLF
ISBN 978-1-50671-203-1
Ariel accidentally drops a bracelet into a cave that supposedly contains a dangerous creature. Her curiosity implores her to enter, and what she finds turns her quest for a bracelet into a quest for truth.

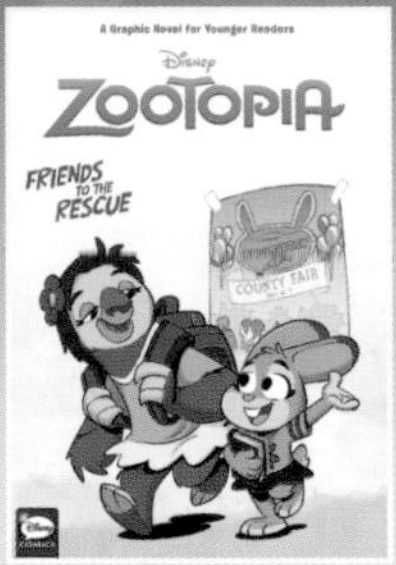

A Graphic Novel for Younger Readers
Disney
ZOOTOPIA
FRIENDS TO THE RESCUE
COUNTY FAIR

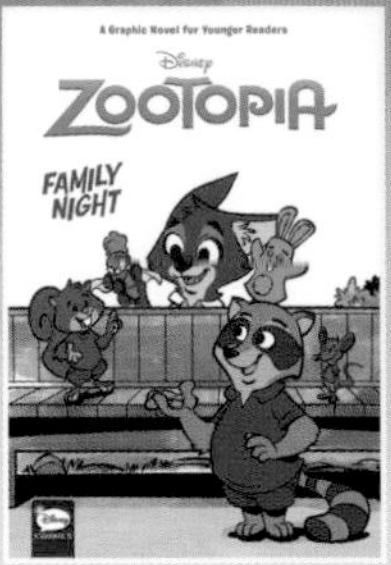

A Graphic Novel for Younger Readers
Disney
ZOOTOPIA
FAMILY NIGHT

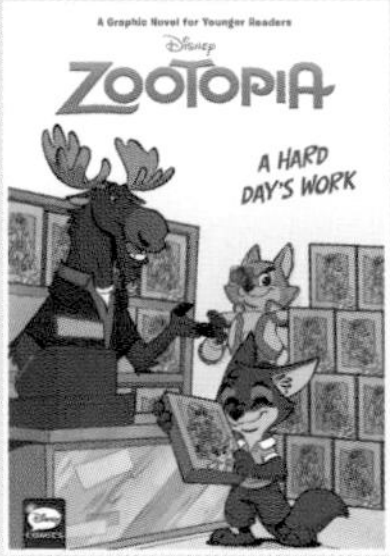

A Graphic Novel for Younger Readers
Disney
ZOOTOPIA
A HARD DAY'S WORK

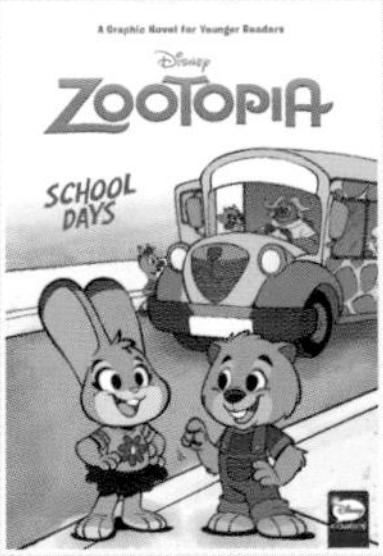

A Graphic Novel for Younger Readers
Disney
ZOOTOPIA
SCHOOL DAYS

DISNEY ZOOTOPIA: FRIENDS TO THE RESCUE
ISBN 978-1-50671-054-9

DISNEY ZOOTOPIA: FAMILY NIGHT
ISBN 978-1-50671-053-2

DISNEY ZOOTOPIA: A HARD DAY'S WORK
ISBN 978-1-50671-206-2

DISNEY ZOOTOPIA: SCHOOL DAYS
ISBN 978-1-50671-205-5

Join young Judy Hopps as she uses wit and bravery to solve mysteries, conundrums, and more! And quick-thinking young Nick Wilde won't be stopped from achieving his goals—where there's a will, there's a way!

AVAILABLE AT YOUR LOCAL COMICS SHOP OR BOOKSTORE! TO FIND A COMICS SHOP IN YOUR AREA, VISIT COMICSHOPLOCATOR.COM

For more information or to order direct, visit DarkHorse.com